The Jack Within

By Jim Shaw

Illustrated by

Jonathan Clark
&
Lois Webster

Copyright © 2023 by Jim Shaw

thejackwithinallofus@yahoo.com

All rights reserved. No part of this publication may be stored in a retrieval system, transmitted in any form or by any means, or reproduced by any means, including photocopying, except for brief excerpts for the purposes of a literary review, without the prior written permission of the author.

ISBN 979-8-9880217-04

Printed in the USA

Preface

I'm not sure what causes a person to have gifts and talents. Obviously the brain is wired in a way that predisposes them to naturally have a proclivity toward doing something other people find appealing. Some people play music, some draw and paint. Others may have a gift to treat and heal the sick. Ultimately, the worthiness of your gift is how much other people find value in it.

My enjoyment for spinning a tale may not be a gift or a talent as this is my first attempt at subjecting this material to public view. So the value of what other people think has yet to be determined. I can say that my family and friends have encouraged me to take this journey to bring you these stories. I certainly don't question the loyalty and support they have given me. I do wonder how much of their beloved advice is due in part to natural prejudice. Either way I am grateful and blessed.

The collection of short stories presented here are but a mild attempt to sooth my overactive imagination. I get these strong feelings and intuitions about things that occupy my idle thinking and they don't go away until I write them down. I've heard musicians say similar things about writing music. I hope that you find some redeeming value in the compulsion to dump my soul onto paper. If just one of these stories has taken you on a walk back in time, or has touched your heart, or has caused you to think… Then sharing them with you was worth writing them down.

When you begin your own personal journey with this book, you will discover a character by the name of Jack. He is the protagonist you will come to know very well with each story you read. I suspect you already know Jack. I think we all have a Jack in our lives to one extent or another. I suspect he may exist to you as parts and pieces of many people you have known your entire life. Jack is the moralistic background that naturally exists in the fabric of our culture. Maybe even in the fabric of each of us. Jack is that quiet, unassuming voice of calm and reason that has influenced all of us at one time or another and we are the better for it.

Please note, every story has been written in a unique style with a little vernacular that Jack uses. That vernacular may seem odd to you and maybe a little hard to read at times, but it is the way Jack talks. Well-meaning editors have tried to "streamline" and "correct" the way Jack says things. I've been told he uses too many words to spit out what he is saying and that his sentence structure is sometimes backward. He may use local expressions and colloquialisms unfamiliar to folks not correctly regionally situated to hear and understand such expressions. But I have refused to give in and sanitize the way Jack says things. You get to read it the way it falls out of his mouth... so to speak.

The one common theme that binds all of these stories together is how they all celebrate the essence of being a man. You will read about good fathers, good friends, good neighbors, and about men in general going about the business of being men. Some subjects and themes will be heavy in nature. You may laugh and you may cry. Being a man is not always an easy task. These stories will give you a front row seat to Jack's struggles to make sense of everyday life as various events and circumstances seem to fall out of the sky into his lap. Such is life.

You will read about one of Jack's more difficult journeys when you read *Prayer Meetings*. Likewise, being a father is not always much fun either unless you can use a little humor to calm your nerves as you will discover in *The Value Of Advice*. Sometimes the trials and tribulations men experience in life become too much to handle and you will be exposed to that numbing experience in *A Day of Reckoning*. Just when you think men are not capable of being strong and caring at the same time, then *Poor Religion* and *Good Medicine* will prove you wrong. And if your emotional capacity can stand the roller coaster ride, I'm guessing you will enjoy *In The Life of Jack*. Finally, for those of you who would like to take a fall hunting adventure from the comfort of your easy chair at home; *The Way It Used to Be* and *Perfect in my eyes* will leave you with that experience while also thinking about the influences you have on other people. Sometimes, the ultimate goal is to actually influence others; Jack will have something to say about that with the stories *William* and *The Beauty of Ugly*. Not surprising, just when you have Jack all figured out, don't let *And She Was* slip up on you. Things aren't always as they appear.

My friends and family say, despite my ardent denials, that "I" am Jack. It would be wrong for me to assume that I could ever be as wise, as patient, or thoughtful, or as kind as Jack. But that does not mean as a man I don't aspire to hold myself to Jack's honorable example. This is where Jack would be bashfully humble, and I am.

– Jim Shaw

Foreword

Please accept my warm greetings to everyone that has found their way to this book. I am excited to welcome you to explore the many well written stories you will find here. You are soon to experience tender, heartfelt situations and passionate presentation.

You will also find the uses of old, traditional words and phrases to guide the reader through a series of adventures where you will discover a lovable character by the name of Jack. Jim smartly puts Jack in situations where he is forced to search for answers and deal with unstable and uncomfortable circumstances.

Jack uses gentility, humor, decency, simplicity and a noticeable streak of stubborn pride to expose the best of human nature. Jack's strength to meet the challenges of his life is found in his abiding gifts of faith, hope and love. With these tools he is able to secure peace, tranquility, and joy. You will find yourself cheering for Jack's successes, morning his loses, and will find comfort in his desire to have finality and closer.

I am proud and honored to write this forward for my friend Jim and invite you to explore the fictional world of his imagination. May God forever bless him.

Robert M. Crosby
B.A., M.A.T., M.E.D., M.A.E.

Dedication

There are many people that influence you during the course of your journey through life. Throw in your personal uniqueness and you develop something you recognize as your own identity. I think, with much reflection, it is the people we encounter during the course of our lives that perhaps influence us the most about who we ultimately become as a person. Our need for human interaction and the ability to give and receive love is a strong social construct that changes, molds, builds, and defines how we see the world and how the world sees us. I think Jack intuitively understood this concept.

I humbly offer to you this list of people I want to recognize with my most sincere gratitude. These loving souls have given me their unselfish time, honest feedback, editing advice, harshest critiques, and happy praises during my attempt to bring these stories to life. The fire of their enthusiasm has been my inspiration. Without the love and support of these people, my courage would not have been so bold, my heart would not be as full, my life would not be as meaningful, and this book would not have been written.

Thank you from the bottom of my heart:

- Emily is the epitome of grace and kindness. Always a faithful and dutiful daughter. She has unselfishly given herself to me in support of this endeavor. She is my biggest fan.

- Stephanie is the straight forward pillar of truth and strength. There is no bigger, softer heart underneath. If you want to keep the story real, this daughter will tell you about it. She is my rock.

- A man needs a few true bosom buddies in his life: Roger, Bruce, Mac, Jamie, Jay, Zac, Ronnie, Tyler, Ralph, David, James, Stephany, Randy, Tom, Tommy, and Bob. You guys have contributed greatly to my developmental path to manhood. No doubt this book is the result of your influences on me.

- And very special thanks to a few people that have supported and guided me with their kind and generous love. They have cheered and offered much needed advice along the way. Your influences have meant much to my confidence to push forward with this project: Stephanie, Janice, Donna, Paul, Beverly, Marty, Mom, and my dearly beloved Mildred.

Finally, I must admit that while these stories are fictional, they are bits and pieces of me and other colorful characters I have known throughout my life. In remembrance to these silent contributions, I offer thanks to the many people that have unknowingly stoked the creative process of my imagination. Your essence now lives in a book.

Contents

1 – The Value of Advice 12

2 – A Man's Footprint... 22

3 – William 29

4 – A Day of Reckoning... 47

5 – Poor Religion 54

6 – Good Medicine 65

7 – In The Life Of Jack 76

8 – Prayer Meetings 91

9 – And She Was 100

10 – The Beauty of Ugly 117

11– Perfect In My Eyes 131

12– The Way It Used To Be 150

The Value of Advice

Jack had been noticing for some time that special sparkle in his daughter's eye when her boyfriend came around. They had been dating for two and a half years and had become quite the "cozy" couple. Seeing this kind of familiarity between his daughter and her boyfriend is not what concerned Jack, however. It was the standoffish, sheepish way the boy had been acting all of a sudden that had the seat of Jack's shorts in a bind. Being observant was the only sure-fire way Jack could glean information out of his two daughters when it came to matters of the heart and Jack had gotten good at reading the signs.

The way Jack had it figured, it was only a matter of time before the young man made his move. Sure, his daughter was twenty five, a full grown woman capable of taking care of her own business. But Jack knew his daughter was raised with a traditional sense of decency and decorum and he was willing to bet the prized pig that the road to matrimony would run straight through him. If that young man were going to ask for his daughter's hand in marriage, the boy would first have to ask the old man for permission.

Jack didn't have to wait long to prove his theory correct. He was sitting in the front porch swing enjoying the cool afternoon when he looked up and saw a car coming down the long driveway. In a puff of dust trailing from the dirt road came the familiar little red car Jack had watched many times take his daughter on dates. The car stopped in front of the house and Jack's mouth got dry. He knew the time had come for the meeting he sensed had been drawing near. The young man got out of his car and made his way to the porch steps.

"Good day Mr. Seavers," the young man said with a half smiling, half scared to death look on his face.

"Bout good as any," Jack said with a dry lilt of aggravation in his voice. "She ain't home and won't be back from town for a while." Jack could easily see his disgruntled nature was having the desired effect on the boy, he appeared to be sweating and he damn near could not speak without trembling. Jack figured the cotton ball in the boy's mouth must be twice the size as the one he was chewing.

"Um- I, I'm…. I've come to see you Mr. Seavers."

Creases in the corners of Jack's mouth devilishly turned upward. A feeling of pity washed over his mood and Jack found himself feeling apologetic for being difficult to approach. Still the same, Jack was not ready to give up on having a little fun. If

Jack was to soon gain a son-in-law, the chap might as well learn to get along in this family. That included having to deal with the old man.

"Son, you better come up here and sit down. You look like you are about to throw-up. I don't know what you could possible want with me? Compared to my daughter, I'm a might near rough to look at, too opinionated for casual conversation, and on occasion have been accused of smelling bad." Jack said, noticing exasperation befall the boy's expression.

The young man stepped onto the porch and sat in a wicker chair across from the old man. He chose a chair near the steps and sat on the edge of his seat in a forward leaning position with his elbows draped across his knees. The boy was as tense as a rubberband and Jack was sure he was on the verge of wetting his pants. The lad was well positioned to run at the first sign of trouble and that gleefully amused the old man.

"Well Sir, um, I've been thinking," the boy said. "I've been seeing your daughter now for about two and a half years, we have both finished college, we both have started dependable careers, and I was thinking that maybe we should start planning a future together. I was hoping that, you… I was wondering if… If, if I could… "

"Hold on a minute boy," Jack interrupted with determined purpose. "It sounds to me like you have been practicing that speech a long time. And it sounds an awful lot like a speech that if it took this much effort and preparation must be about something important. You rest your bones in that chair and I'll be right back."

Without saying another word, Jack stood up and disappeared inside the house. The boy was not yet used to Jack's rough exterior and it made him feel mindful that his life could be in a delicate balance at any moment. Even by the usual standards of rough and gruff the old man was extra scary today. Maybe Jack's scariness was magnified by the fact the boy was without his girlfriend to use as a human shield should the conversation turn sour.

He respected Jack for being a man's man but also knew Jack to be nothing but attentive and loving where his daughters were concerned. There were many times he had seen Jack lift one of those large calloused hands into the air and land it on the head of one of those girls with such a gentle stroke of caring that one would think those callouses were large, fluffy marshmallows. The girls would always smile and lean their head into Jack's hand to receive the affection.

"Okay, so the man has a soft spot," the boy thought. But that still does not change the fact that HE was not exactly the apple of Jack's eye and just why Jack needed to go inside the house was now starting to cause the lackey much concern. The young man sat restless and repositioned himself in the chair many times while hearing heavy footsteps pacing back and forth on the hardwood floor. The boy's imagination started to wonder and he became curious to know at what lengths would a man of Jack's rugged, no nonsense nature go to when deciding to protect his daughter from a young gentleman caller aiming to take his little girl away? At that very moment, Jack kicked the screened door open with his foot and the young man instinctively jumped to his feet.

"Boy, you got up so fast you left some of your britches in that chair. Sit down and finish your story." Jack said.

The young man was relieved to see that Jack had gotten two heavy glass tumblers and a bottle of his finest bourbon instead of the shotgun. Jack sat everything on a table near the swing. The boy started his speech over again and this time he spoke naturally with unrehearsed words, "Sir, I love your daughter very much. She is the most wonderful woman I've ever known. And while I know I could never take your place in her heart, I would spend my life trying to have a small piece of it. I would very much like to ask your daughter to marry me and I am asking for your permission to do so."

There was a long uncomfortable silence. Jack arranged the tumblers on the stand and poured two shots of the brown liquor. He picked up the tumblers and gave the boy one and said, "I think we need a drink. It is not every day a man wanders into a lion's den and expects to get out with his hide intact." The young man cocked his head back and tilted the heavy glass with a quick jerk and swallowed. The bourbon burned all the way down and seemed to evaporate the air in his throat and lungs causing him to cough while trying to catch his breath at the same time. As soon as it was humanly possible to catch his breath with scorched vocal cords, the boy said, "But Sir…"

Jack quickly cut him off again with a mater-of-fact tone in his voice, "It's not me you need to be scared of boy, it's that woman you think you want to marry. Did you bring your lion tamer's suit?"

Jack was standing over the seated boy looking down on him

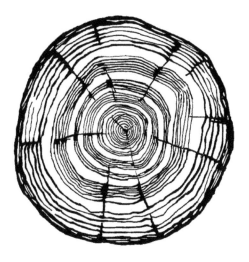

while dispensing wisdom, "Son, I know a thing or two about young love. I also know there isn't a damn thing I can tell you that will change those feeling you are having. And, if she will have you, there's nothing I can do to stop either of you from doing whatever it is you set your mind to. I have spent the best part of my life learning to live among the felines and carry the scars to prove it." Jack reached out and took the tumbler from the boy's hand and poured themselves another shot. He handed the loaded glass back to the boy and gave an open-air nod toward the boy with his own glass, and hammered back the shot with experience.

The boy took big gulp and went into another coughing fit. Jack pretended not to notice and continued with his lecture. Jack said, "I wish there was a way to open up your head and pour in the knowledge you will need to prepare you for married life. But there is no easy way to learn this information except to learn by experience. Young men are naturally blinded by love and the allure of a woman. It is Mother Nature's way of perpetuating the human species."

"But Sir," the boy protested. "I see your wonderful relationship with your daughters and have dreamed about how wonderful it would be to have a family of my own. Is it not all worth it?"

The boy did have a point. And it's not like Jack was really trying to discourage the boy from his quest in the first place. Jack wanted to make clear to the boy that a lifelong commitment of marriage was no honeymoon, even though it starts out that way.

The liquor had started working on the young man and he was beginning to feel more relaxed. Jack thought this would be a good time to have some more fun. "Sounds like you have thought this engagement thing through, if you don't mind me ask'n, what's your back up plan?" Jack said with a wiry grin and a squint in his eye.

"Excuse me Sir, I am lost in this conversation. What is a backup plan and why do I need one?" The boy said with genuine confusion written all over his face.

"My boy, has your father not taught you anything? Every young man making a proposal of marriage must be prepared to pay the price. Are you prepared to pay?" The old man asked.

"Sir, are you asking for a dowry?" The boy questioned.

Jack poured each of them another shot and pretended to be outraged by the young man's lack of knowledge concerning the serious business at hand. "Did you not insinuate a few minutes ago that my daughter was a real dandy of a catch?" Jack said as if to accuse him of treason. "If that is true, then you must first make sure the engagement ring is some more fancy. You know a woman has a good idea how much she is worth. I, myself, have always suspected their self-appraisal running a little on the high side.

And then you must have the back-up deal clinchers just to make sure you have enough clout to cover the cost of her self-appraisal should the ring fall a little short of her expectation. Some men will also have in their back pocket at the critical moment a little insurance. Maybe a couple three day cruise tickets, or matching earrings, or some other really nice something to offer her if you see she is hesitant about making you a solid commitment. Some girls are really good at hem-hawing around to get the extra stuff, you following me boy?"

"No Sir, I'm still really confused. What deal are we clenching exactly? And, can you give me a clue as to this 'self-value philosophy' you are talking about?" The boy said, now sipping his drink with a little less discomfort.

"Look son, it's like this, an engagement of marriage is like a bribe. You got to bribe the girl with diamonds and expensive gifts to get her attention. Do you really think you can convince a woman to committing the rest of her life to a cheap bastard who's only offering for her lifelong commitment is a ring from a gumball machine and no back-up plan? Love is a dollar bill deep and a dime short. Women say they would never put a price on love. Well, that's true only because you can never get one of them to admit it. Stand back and watch as her girlfriends get together and aw over the ring you give her. Bigger the ring, bigger the fuss they make over it. Tell me that kind of behavior is not evidence enough pointing out the validity of what I'm saying. Highway robbery is all. Let me ask you a question, just how much money or expensive gifts are YOU expecting to get out of this engagement deal?"

"Sir, I would never expect anything except your daughter's love," the boy said as he slammed the empty glass down on the chair arm emphasizing his sincerity.

"Exactly my point," Jack said with conviction. "You are young, inexperienced and doomed to pay a life penance for your short sightedness. A woman's love is a fickle thing. You will watch her selflessly give love and energy to everyone around her every day, all day long and hand you the leftover scraps at night. It's how they, dare I say it out loud… keep a man in line. You see, a woman's love is what she wants it to be, if she wants it to be anything at all. And what of it she decides to give to you is all you're going to get, and YOU will be thankful to get it." Jack paused long enough to pour another round, a double, and handed the glass back to the boy.

"What you will soon figure out is that a woman is what she is and she won't be anything more or less. You may wish for her to be this or that, but you will find yourself hard pressed to hold her accountable for her short comings because you'll know deep down it really is not her fault, she is just being a woman. You can learn to love them for the way they are, or run from them. Either way is going to hurt a little and you're likely to get scratched and skinned up a bit in the process." Jack mused as he poured the boy another drink.

With drooping eyes and slurred words, the boy asked Jack, "Mithter Sevvvers, tell mee a'gin bout bribrery'n da woman to maarry."

Jack was about finished having fun with the boy and was going to let him off the hook of being teased when he looked up and saw his daughters coming down the driveway from their day in town. "Look boy, here comes the girls. You got to promise me you will never open your mouth about our conversation today. You got to promise! Suck down that last drink. Hurry boy, hurry, they're almost here."

Jack looked like the cat that had swallowed the canary when his daughters stepped onto the porch. One look at the situation and the girls easily recognized that Jack had taken advantage of the unsuspecting and inexperienced young man. Both girls gave their father the evil eye and a scornful rebuke for rendering the gentleman befuddled. Jack told his daughter, "Go put the boy on the sofa and let him sleep a bit. I don't think he is feeling very well." But just before the boy went inside the house with his arm wrapped around his girlfriend's neck leaning on her for stability, he stopped to ask Jack one last question, "Sirr, will'ya teeeach me how'ta geet thru it?"

Jack fondly admired the last sip of courage in his own glass, looked at the boy and simply replied, "I just did."

A Man's Footprint

Cole didn't mind being left alone in Grandpa's house, even though it was an odd feeling. The house felt cold and empty unlike the usual happy, warm atmosphere Cole usually felt when visiting his Grandpa. He thought it was funny how every home seems to have its own sounds and smells. Cole was surprised when he noticed these unique sounds and smells of Grandpa's kitchen when he had no previous knowledge of their existence before. Loud, noticeable sounds he was sure had always existed. The ticking wall clock over the sink and the refrigerator running with a low hum were surely sounds that had always been present. He was certain of it.

The kitchen also had a faint smell of coffee even though there was no coffee currently available. Cole thought it was possible to miss these kinds of things when you were a runny nose little kid. But at fourteen, Cole thought he was beyond the point of riding the apron strings of his mother or being spoon-fed every little detail of his life. He was beginning to have his own thoughts and ideas. Cole was becoming aware of making his own decisions and life choices.

But in that moment, Cole's thoughts were primarily with his Grandpa. Sitting in a hard kitchen chair, Cole was concerned about him and felt a sense of relief that his mother was going to be with Grandpa for the day. Cole was not exactly sure why Grandpa was in the hospital, only that he was sick and that his mother was very concerned. Cole could tell his mother was being a little evasive about Grandpa's condition and he could tell she was worried more than she was willing to admit as if hiding from the truth somehow made it better.

Cole had never seen his mother worry so much. Her face was pale and looked drawn with her lips pursed tight. Her eyes were sad with what looked like a million miles of distance behind them. Worry was even present in her voice as she spoke using few but direct words to communicate. Cole hated seeing his mother nervously wrapped in her emotions. She appeared to need comforting and he didn't feel like he had enough of whatever it would take to make her feel better. He got the feeling that no one was capable of giving her comfort, with maybe the exception of Grandpa.

Even Cole cold see those two had a close relationship; and Cole was maybe a bit jealous at times the way they would happily banter between themselves at the exclusion of others no matter how much time separated their visits. It was weird how Cole's mother always seemed to be peaceful and content when in Grandpa's company. Grandpa would call her "his little girl" and she would always smile when he did. Grandpa said she would always be "his little girl," and he would say it with boastful pride as if admiring a precious gem. She grew up being a daddy's girl no doubt it.

Cole wandered through the house in search of the television. His mothers' instructions were to make himself at home because she would probably be gone the entire day. He was not sure what would be on daytime TV, but it had to be better than the lonesome feeling he was enduring sitting in the kitchen.

Cole had to walk past the den as he went down the hall toward the living room. The den was a restricted room. His mother told him loaded guns could be in the room and to never enter without parental guidance. Cole would have probably never thought about Grandpa's room if the door had not been half open already. Grandpa once said he had to keep the door closed because it was a mess inside and it made the rest of the house look untidy. Cole could never remember a time when the door was open, even when Grandpa was inside.

Standing at the den door, Cole gently pushed the door open all the way. He expected the room to be a cluttered mess as he was previously warned, but he could plainly see the room was extremely organized and clean. Cole's mother made him do chores around their home; often enough for him to have a clear appreciation for what clean really looked like. The clean, organized room impressed Cole and he stepped inside nodding his head in approval looking around like he was in charge of inspecting the place.

Immediately Cole's senses were engaged. His eyes feasted on

the vast adornment of sporting memorabilia terrifically manicured in every available void. His nose picked up the scent of apple wood pipe tobacco and gun oil. The mixture of smells was pleasing to him. Cole had never really contemplated what a manly smell should be like, but he easily determined these smells were not of a feminine creation.

Cole remembered the few times he previously went into the room on the heels of his Grandpa. He was much younger and they were only brief incidences. Certainly not the kind of encounter that would prepare him for the awesome, breathtaking amount of life and energy that was now emanating from the room. There were mounted game heads of all kinds wearing huge sets of antlers. There were stuffed ducks, turkeys, and pheasants hanging from the walls and sitting on the tables. There were fine specimens of salt water and fresh water fish captured in various poses. Turkey calls, duck decoys, old wood fishing lures and paper shot shells were scattered around the room. Cole found the artwork hanging on the walls to be intriguing. They depicted scenes of old barns, homesteads, and landscapes of long ago rural country living. A few of the paintings had a rough texture and Cole wondered if they were original works of art.

The room was a treasure trove waiting discovery. Everywhere Cole looked he found something new and interesting to examine. The duck leg bands wrapped around a lanyard holding a beat-up duck call was neat. There was a book shelf full of books. Most of them seemed to be about the old west, or about hunting and fishing. They looked like old books likely from the yester-years of his Grandpa's life. Most of the books were leather bound and richly embossed with the title and the author's name. Some of the books had hunting scenes depicted on the front covers.

Cole found Grandpa's felt hat interesting as it was adorned with wild turkey spurs strung on a leather boot string. The collection of spurs was wrapped around the hat apparently serving as a hat band. There were also a few small turkey feathers stuck in the left side.

Cole was careful to examine only one thing at a time and made sure to put it back the way he found it. The more he poked around in the room the more interesting items he discovered. But Cole only felt comfortable looking at the stuff that was clearly on display. He respected his Grandpa's privacy enough not to go digging into anything that was closed or out of sight. Cole could only imagine the cool stuff that could be tucked away in the knotty pine wardrobe on the left side of the room, or the cedar hope chest in front of the desk, or the walnut chest of drawers behind the door. There was even a wood case under the window that housed many small doors and drawers. The room even had a closet. Surely many treasures awaiting discovery could be found in there. Cole was extremely tempted to look inside the closet but reminded himself of his rule not to open anything closed.

Finally, Cole pulled out the chair at the desk and sat down. From the captain's seat, Cole had a clear view of everything. It was as though the entire room had been decorated from the view of the chair. But what really caught his attention were the many framed photographs scattered across the desk top. They were mostly family themed photos capturing hunting and outdoor scenes. Cole laughed seeing pictures of his mother as a baby and little girl. Some pictures were of his mother and his aunt together with captions written across the pictures saying things such as: "Cleaning Daddy's turkey," and "First time in a duck blind." Cole was told about how his mother grew up a tomboy. And he had heard stories about her tomboy adventures living in the country and growing up on a farm. To Cole, his mother did not outwardly appear to show any signs of this kind of life existing within her. Until now, he had never grasped the  significance of this part of her life and he was a little surprised realizing how little he actually knew about his mother.

Cole sat for a long time behind the desk staring at the pictures. Each picture depicted action, success, adventure, and most of all…happiness. There was genuine happiness in every picture unlike the fake smiles and board looks he was used to seeing in the family type photos at his house.

In contrast, Cole thought about the worried look his mother had when she left this morning. He realized now how deep his mother's concerns must have been and how important Grandpa was to her. Cole now understood that growing up a tomboy in the footsteps of his Grandpa left an indelible mark on his mother after all. Tears welled in his eyes thinking about how worried she looked this morning and the hurt she must be feeling. Cole was feeling guilty for not having gone to the hospital with her. But she wanted him to stay at the house in case other family members dropped by. Cole felt a bulging, painful sense of duty building in his chest. He wanted so much to be with her at that moment as if he now felt more prepared and capable of comforting her somehow.

Cole looked around the room and felt a tremendous weight fall upon his shoulders. He no longer saw mere trinkets and keepsakes, but the bold identity and rich flavor of a man's life. Cole never realized what being a man looked like. And until now, he had never contemplated what being a man felt like. But it became very clear to him that his Grandpa was the kind of man he hoped to be. Cole wanted to be a strong man with diverse interest and a unique dedication to family and to live an honest, respectable way of life. And if the measure of being a man could be found in the strong, loving, caring, and dependable bonds he forged with family and friends, there was no doubt in Cole's mind that Grandpa was a great man.

William

"I HATE YOU; I HATE YOU!!!" shouted the young man.

"You are not exactly the person at the top of my Christmas list either." Jack replied.

"Then why are you holding me hostage here? This is kidnapping and you are going to be in big trouble," came yet another insult from the boy thrown at Jack.

"You can leave anytime you want. There are no bars on the windows and the doors don't even have locks. The way I figure it, the sooner you get started walking, the sooner you will get where it is you want to go." Jack said.

"I don't know the way. Besides, you brought me here now you must take me home! The boy exclaimed confidently.

"If you walk down this long driveway to the main road, you can take a right or left, either way is acceptable, and then walk another 5 miles or so, then you will be somewhere. See, leaving is not that difficult. As for me taking you someplace, I am not doing anything for you unless you deserve it. Right now, the only thing you deserve from me is a switch on your backside." Jack quipped, starting to sound a little short tempered.

The boy said, "That is child abuse if you touch me. You will go to jail for that."

To which Jack replied with a smug smile, "Son, the sheriff of this county hunts my farm. We went to high school together. To say we are great friends and go way back is an understatement. Tell you what, how about we call him. I would be willing to bet he would volunteer to watch me tan your backside just to make sure I did a thorough enough job of it once I tell him how you have been acting."

Exasperated, the young man stormed off to the bedroom he had been given to use without saying another word.

Bo was not the name his mother had given him. That name was William. Somehow over the years, things got shortened to Bo. So, that is what Jack called him. Bo had been kicked out of school for fighting and being uncontrollable and disrespectful. His mother, Mary, was Jack's brother's, wife's, sister. And while that was not exactly what Jack would call close family, Jack listened to her problem just the same. Mary had called Jack for advice about what to do with Bo and how to help him. She had been trying to handle the escalating situation by herself for a long time but his being expelled from school was the final straw. She could no longer control the young man and was exhausted and defeated. After listening to Mary explain things, Jack was beginning to think modifying Bo's behavior sounded like a man size job.

That is the beginning of how Jack became involved, but it is not as though Jack did not have a say in the decision about whether or not he wanted to help. Jack more or less volunteered for the job upon hearing the desperation in Mary's voice. Jack was a sucker for helping people, but it was not Mary he was inspired to help. It was that young man that Jack wanted to set straight. The world was full of thieves and thugs and the last thing Jack wanted was yet another menace set loose on society.

Jack told Mary that he would take the boy for a while to see if fresh air and clean, country living wouldn't do the young man some good. Jack did not have to work too hard talking Mary into accepting his offer to help. She was an overwhelming, willing participant to say the least. But before Jack took on the job to reform Bo, he encouraged Mary to stay away and let him do things his way. Mary trusted Jack and readily handed the boy over.

It didn't take long for the boy to return to the living room where Jack sat reading a book. The boy spoke first, "How long am I going to be here?"

"Until," Jack said.

"Until what? Until is no answer," The boy responded.

Jack looked inquisitive and said, "Really, how so?"

The boy was quick to point out, "Until is not specific. I want to know if I am going be here over night, for a couple of days, or a week?"

Jack appeared to give the boy some credit for his inquiry, especially since he was asking the question in a pleasant tone. Jack said, "I suppose you are correct. The word by itself is not terribly descriptive. But if you include the word into a sentence, then it does reflect more meaning. How about this, UNTIL I SAY SO. There, does that clear things up for you?"

The boy huffed with an attitude. "That still does not tell me anything. I want to go home and I want to go home now."
"And you plan to do what exactly when you get home?" You aren't in school anymore, you don't go to church, you are only

thirteen years old so you don't drive and cannot get a job. Just what do you plan to do when you get there?" Jack asked.

The boy was quick to respond, "I have friends. I can play games. I can ride my bike. There is a lot I can do at home. Besides, I don't like you and there is nothing to do around here."

Jack did not take the bait of being drawn into an argument that had no meaningful outcome. Instead, he talked calmly while keeping his eyes looking into his book pretending to read while he spoke. "Son, I guess doing things and finding meaning in them is a matter of perspective. You need to have some perspective."

"Uggg…I hate this. I hate talking to you. You don't say things so I can understand them. Why do you have to be so difficult? You are just an old man, you don't know shit about nothing."

As gentle as a feather, Jack closed his book and put it on the table beside his chair. He eased from the chair slowly but deliberately. It only took Jack four quick steps before reaching the boy sitting on the sofa. With one swift motion, Jack grabbed Bo by his shirt collar and snatched him into the air so that the boy and Jack were now nose to nose. The boy's feet were not touching the floor. Jack looked straight into the boy's eyes and said in a commanding voice, "You are way too young to cuss and I am way too old not to be respected. I suggest you go to your room for the night. Otherwise, snatching you off this sofa will be the least of what I do to you."

Jack let the boy go with a little forward thrust and the boy hit the floor with a thud. Jack turned and went to his own room and shut the door leaving the boy looking dazed and confused.

The next morning, Jack filled the house with the smell of coffee and frying bacon. There was also grits, eggs, toast, fresh milk, and some of the best fig preserves this side of the Mississippi. Jack was humming to himself when he heard a noise from the kitchen table. It was a chair being pulled out as Bo was taking a seat. The table was not set. It was just an empty table with a disheveled, empty looking little boy sitting at the far end.

Jack turned and spoke to the boy, "Say, did you sleep well last night?"

"No, the bed is hard. I did not sleep good at all. I kept waking up. And early this morning, loud crowing chickens wouldn't shut up."

"That's alright, you will get used to it." Jack assured him. "Here you go son, come get a plate and fix yourself some of this breakfast. It's not much good cold."

The boy did not say anything, but hearing Jack say that he would get used to the small, uncomfortable bed and the persistent chicken racket every morning gave the boy some indication he should expect to be there for a long time. And while he still may not have liked being at the farm, having some idea about the duration of his fate brought some resolve to his spirit. That… and the hunger pains in his stomach squashed all desire to be rebellious at the moment.

Breakfast was quiet between Jack and the boy, but not uncomfortably so. Jack was preoccupied with reading the local newspaper and the boy was too busy eating. Young boys are naturally hungry. Breakfast was good and the boy cleaned his plate.

"Bo," Jack announced, "I was the cook, so you can be the dishwasher. We will share the chores around here."

"But I don't know how to wash dishes," Said the boy.

"That's alright. I can show you how the first time," Jack said. "And by the way... can you cook?"

"No! I cannot cook," was the quick reply.

"Good! Not sure I really wanted to eat your cooking in the first place. Well then, you may want to get good at dishwashing. If I am to do all the cooking, then you will be doing all the dishwashing." Jack informed him in a straightforward manner.

The boy opened his mouth to speak just as Jack gave him a look of authority. Bo quickly choked down the automated smart-assed response getting ready to spew forth. Bo was not looking to stir Jack up again so soon after their encounter from the night before.

"As for chores, Jack said, there is a lot to do today. Finish your breakfast and let's see about getting those dishes done. Then you go wash your face, brush your teeth and get dressed. Don't worry about putting on your best Sunday clothes. The chores we will be doing today will require utility not fashionable presentation."

Now reader, you know what happens next. Yep, Jack spent

the day working the young man as hard as he could push him. They spent the morning feeding and tending to the farm animals. There were chickens, cows, goats, an old mule that stayed near the barn, two hogs in their own pen out in the pasture, and two dogs that followed them everywhere they went. They mended two areas of barbed wired fencing that had come loose. They worked on putting a few new blades on the hay cutting machine. They changed the oil in the big diesel tractor. And to end the day, Jack started the boy on the wood pile with an axe. Something about chopping wood will make a man think clearly about his circumstances.

By the time Jack called the boy into the house for supper, he was exhausted. Bo was not used to being physically active. The only thing keeping Bo from total collapse was his youth. Everything else had given up. His feet hurt. He had blisters on his hands. His shoulders and back ached and he was just too tired to care about anything else.

After supper, Jack felt sorry for the boy, but made him do the dishes anyway. Jack told the boy when he complained, "If you want to be a man, then you have to first stop being a free loading kid. You have to learn how to shoulder responsibilities. A man never shirks his responsibilities. Those dishes are your responsibility."

The boy failed to see value in what Jack was saying, but he knew if he was going to soon get to sit and rest a minute, he was gonna have to first wash those dishes. And he did.

Bo made his way to the living room where Jack had started a fire in the fireplace. Jack was sitting in his chair holding the book he had been reading. Except for a small reading lamp next to Jack's chair, the room was lit only by the warm yellow glow from the fire. The young man sat on the sofa near the fire. He could feel the warmth on his legs and face. The burning wood made crackling sounds as the flames lapped at the logs in an effort to consume them. The aroma of burning wood was a new smell to Bo. He liked it and was soon fast asleep.

Bo woke the next morning to the smell of bacon and coffee. The fire had gone out and the room had a chill. But there had been a blanket thrown over him, for which he was grateful. The exuberant expectation of eating breakfast became a distant thought as the boy tried to move. To say that every muscle in his body hurt was a vast understatement. Jack heard a moan and noticed the boy trying to raise himself to a sitting position. He knew what the boy was experiencing and grew a devilish smile.

With a tone of urgency, Jack called to the boy, "Son, you best come get some of this breakfast before the dogs beat you to it."

"I cannot move Jack. I am sick. I hurt all over and need to go to the Doctor," the boy said with genuine concern.

"What you need are two aspirin and another healthy dose of

that axe to work out the soreness," Jack exclaimed. "Now come get some breakfast before I eat it all."

The hunger rumbling in Bo's belly was stronger than his will to protest. Defiantly and with great pain he made his way to the table. Once seated, Jack took enough pity on the boy to fix his plate for him. Jack figured it was the least he could do for the boy given his circumstances.
"How did you sleep? Did that uncomfortable sofa and those pesky chickens keep you awake?" Jack asked the boy.

"I guess not. I don't remember. I don't even remember falling asleep. All I remember is waking up just now on the living room sofa with a blanket wrapped around me." The boy said.

"A hard day's work is good for a man. It causes him to eat hardy and sleep deep. Hard work will also keep a man's mind focused on the things that are truly important in life." Jack reminded the boy.

"What did we do that was important yesterday?" The boy wanted to know.

"Let's see, Jack postulated. How did you like breakfast this morning? Were the eggs good? They must have been, you wolfed them down and got seconds. You gathered those eggs yesterday from the hen house. I would think harvesting the food that keeps you alive would be considered important. And that cozy fire that kept you warm and put you to sleep last night was a result of you splitting those logs in order to have that fire in the first place. Actually, everything we did yesterday was very important to the overall plan of living life on this farm.

Everything we did had a purpose for keeping us fed, alive and well." Jack said.

"Is that what you mean by having responsibilities?" The boy questioned.

Jack smiled at the boy. "Now you are catching on. Sometimes your responsibilities aren't always easy to see or understand as to why they are important. Say you don't wash the dishes. You may not think washing the dishes will have direct consequences to your wellbeing. However it does, because if you don't wash the dishes then you have broken your trust with me to share the chores. Then I don't cook for you. I can wash my own dishes, but you cannot cook. Guess that makes dishwashing an awfully important responsibility for you after all or else you will starve."

"You have to feed me. You are responsible for me." The boy pointed out.

After a short but noticeable pause, Jack lamented, "no, I am not responsible for you. You are responsible for yourself. What happens to you is a direct result of how you conduct yourself. My responsibility is to my neighbors, to the people in town, and your mother to ensure that you will grow up to be a respectful, responsible citizen and not a low life crackhead looking to push down old ladies for their social security checks."

"So I'm a crack head now?" The boy was quick to respond.

"Let me ask you a question," Jack asked. "Do you think a respectable, responsible young man would have gotten himself thrown out of school? Just as your actions have consequences here on the farm, so do they have consequences out in the real world. You are responsible for the treatment you receive. No one owes you anything and nothing in life is free. The sooner you come to realize the importance of what I just said the sooner you will understand these things I am trying to teach you." The boy sat looking at his empty plate. He did not grasp the full nature of what Jack had to say. But he was learning a lot about how his actions and behavior determined how he was treated. The boy was thoughtful when he spoke, he asked Jack, "Do you think my mother still loves me?"

The boy's question was not out of place but did catch Jack by surprise. Jack saw the question as a sign the boy might be softening up a little. Jack simply responded, "Son, the reason you are here is because she loves you." The boy sat quietly at the table and looked up at Jack bashfully. No other words were exchanged between them.

In the blink of an eye, six weeks had passed. The boy had grown accustomed to life on the farm and soon learned the daily routine of tending to the animals, and other chores that had to be done. As usual, every day always ended on top of the wood pile with the axe. Farm life has a way of changing a person's perspective about things and Jack liked the changes he was seeing with Bo.

However, today was going to be different, Jack needed supplies from town and he was going to take Bo with him. This was to be a dry run for Bo to see how the changes he was making living on the farm transferred to regular everyday life elsewhere with other people. Jack had some reservations whether or not the boy was ready but there was only one way to find out.

The boy seemed overjoyed upon hearing about going to town. He ran into the bathroom to clean up after morning chores, put on clean clothes, and announced to Jack he was ready to go. Jack was sitting at the kitchen table when Bo made his appearance. The first thing Jack noticed about the boy was the huge smile he had wedged between his ears. After that, there wasn't much else to celebrate. Jack felt bad for not noticing sooner, but young boys grow fast. A lot had changed about Bo in six weeks and not just his attitude. He needed a haircut something terrible. His pants legs were high watered way above his ankles. The few clothes Bo did have were all that he initially brought with him, so they had endured the treachery of farm life and suffered the consequences. Rips, tears, and stains of all kinds that would not come clean anymore had added to the dilapidated look of the young man. Jack felt awful about letting the boy get to this state of looking unkempt, but the boy did not seem to care.

Jack's first stop in town was the general store. Jack marched the boy through the front doors, straight past the counter and up the stairs to where all the clothes were on display. "Mable?!" Jack called out. Mable was the lady in charge of this department and came running to see what was so urgent in Jack's tone. "Mable, this here is Bo, he is staying out at my place for a while. I need you to outfit him with some clothes please." Jack explained. "Get him something to wear for the farm, and some boots, and a hat if he wants one. And then dress him in a going to town outfit, something casually fashionable for young men now-a-days."

Mable didn't even acknowledge Jack with words. She and Jack had been friends a long time and she knew what she needed to do. Nodding at Jack as she walked past, Mable took the boy by the arm and led him down the aisle toward the section that would likely have his size.

An hour later, Mable presented Bo to Jack who was sitting downstairs by the wood burning stove reading the newspaper. Like magic, the boy had been transformed into a very nice looking young man. Jack was impressed.

Mable said to Jack with biting contempt, "Jack, you owe me a big favor for helping you out of this one. How could you have let this poor boy get into such rough shape? I had to throw away all of his other clothes including the shoes, there was nothing to salvage."

Jack sheepishly nodded in agreement, "I will make it up to you with your tip." Jack muttered with a bit of aggravation in his tone even though his mood was just for show.

With bags under both arms, Bo walked behind Jack as they left the store. Next on the list of places to visit was the barber shop. Old man James was on duty as always and was glad to see Jack when he walked in. "Good morning James, " Jack called out as he entered the shop.

"Morning Jack, who you got with you?" Asked James smiling.

"Just Bo, he has been staying out at my place. Do you think we could get a couple of haircuts?" Not waiting for an answer, Jack casually took a seat in the empty barber's chair first. "Cut it like always." Jack instructed.
The barber cut both men's hair with care. Being an old fashion barber shop, a straight razor shave came with the haircut. It was the first time the boy's face had ever been shaved. That straight razor cleaned all the baby fuzz off of Bo's chin and upper lip with ease. "Jack," James said, "the boy turned out real nice if I do say so myself." Jack agreed, paid the tab, and out the door they went vowing to be back again in a month or so.

The last stop on Jack's trip to town that did not actually include picking up supplies was lunch at the diner. Stopping at the diner was a luxury for Jack. Not many times did he feel dressed appropriately for civilized folks trying to eat without the looks and smells of a farmer distracting their appetite. But this day was special because he was proud to be showing off his friend Bo.

The pair took a seat at one of the booths next to the front windows. Jack liked looking outside while he ate. The waitress was a cute, mid-thirties, blond with a bubbly personality. She greeted Jack with pencil and pad ready to take their order saying, "Jack you know the drill, on the blackboard are three meats and six side items listed today, pick a meat and two sides and I will bring it right out."

After ordering, Jack said to the waitress, "Vickie, this is my friend William. He is staying out at my place for a while." William began blushing not used to having attention drawn to him. He gave a bashful smile to Vickie but was too shy to speak. Vickie asked Jack, "Where did you pick him up, he is a cutie?" Jack simply gave a prideful look toward the boy.

Once Vickie was safely out of earshot, Bo asked Jack why he called him William, wondering if Jack had lost some of his marbles. Jack looked at the boy and simply asked, "Did you want to pick a fight with Vickie?" The boy looked perplexed. Jack also asked the boy if he wanted to fight James or Mable? Still unclear what point Jack was trying to make, the boy sat quietly, seriously looking confused.

Jack said, "Son, the snotty nosed kid I knew as Bo does not exist anymore. Sitting before me is a courteous, handsome young man I am proud to have by my side. I hope you have learned much over these past few weeks. As a man, during the course of your life, you will have mighty physical power and strength but will never use it for evil. You will have a busy life, but will stop to help other people along the way. You are smart, but it will be known by how other people speak of you not how you talk about yourself. You will earn respect by giving it. You will treat people with kindness knowing your only reward will be an appreciative smile. You will be responsible for your fair share of the chores in life but will do a little extra just because you can. And the next time you have to fight, it will be because mean and hateful people have backed you into a corner leaving you no other option. A young man of your new and improved stature needs to have a respectful name that announces to the world that you are a man of honor and character. Your mother named you William. It is time for you to claim your rightful birth name, and with it, all the hopes and dreams your mother had for you when she gave you that name. It is time for you to be the man you were meant to be. The kind of man that will make your mother proud instead of ashamed of you."

Jack's words made William smile and a sense of overwhelming pride and self-confidence washed over him.

"We have one more bit of business to handle here in town today." Jack said pointing to the telephone hanging on the wall. Jack instructed, "I want you to call your best friend. I want you to explain how you have been away at an uncle's farm these past few weeks and that you are coming home tomorrow and would like some help painting the backyard fence. Trust me, this may be the most important lesson I teach you."

Jack pushed a dime across the table toward William. William got up and dialed the number and his friend answered. After a brief general conversation, William asked for help with the fence painting just as Jack had instructed. The friend declined participating stating that he must help his mom around their house all day.

After lunch, Jack gave the boy another dime. Jack leaned across the table and whispered, "Call your friend again and this time tell him you have scored some killer weed and want to know if he could come over tomorrow." William trusted Jack. He had grown accustomed to Jack's weird methods of making a point so he did not question his instructions. William delivered the message just as Jack had asked him to do. Instantly, his friend was available all day and wanted to know what time he should come over.

Jack did not need to point out the lesson he was teaching. The point was clear to William that this boy was not a true friend and was using William for his own selfishness. William was glad to end the relationship with this boy. He was going to end all of his old relationships with the people that did not share the same character and moral disposition he was proud to have.

William asked Jack, "How did you know?"

Jack shrugged his shoulders and thoughtfully replied, "Just a hunch, I figured anyone wanting to be friends with Bo was not anyone we would choose to associate with. You have learned to be different now and will no longer seek the morally broken adventures of your youthful past. You are no longer afraid of hard work but see the value in it. You know the difference between right and wrong and have the courage to stand strong for both. You now take pride in being responsible and dependable and will lift folks up instead of shoving them down for their social security checks. You are a real man now and don't you soon forget it."

A Day Of Reckoning

The November day was cold and cloudy. A light but steady rain had been falling with the temperatures hugging just on the south side of freezing. It was the kind of day that seemed to have no meaningful purpose. What was mother-nature thinking to have created such a dreary, miserable day? Even as Jack settled into his comfortable chair in front of the warm fireplace, he felt no comfort.

Staring into the fire watching the flames angrily dance, Jack allowed his mind to wonder aimlessly. An hour passed without meaningful notice and with the exception of pulling a blanket around himself, he did not move. He was still in shock over the news that his long-time friend and hunting partner, Ragan Bennett, had committed suicide.

Jack visited with Ragan's family earlier in the day before the funeral. He feebly tried to offer them kind words of comfort and reassurance to sooth their grieving loss. Jack knew the family well, especially Ragan's brothers and two daughters, but he could not seem to find the right words.

Sitting by the fire he was embarrassed over how he had been such a fumbling tongue tied fool. Jack painfully remembered how he held the daughter's hand trying to console her but instead emotionally tripped over his own discomfort. How the hell was he to provide comfort to the family when he could not hold down his own fragile emotions?

Jack removed his shoes and pointed his feet toward the fire. As he pulled a blanket around his neck, Jack noticed the umbrella standing beside the door and the puddle it made on the floor were almost dry. Seeing the umbrella reminded him of how terrible the weather was outside. It also reminded him of just how terrible he felt inside.

How could Ragan, of all people, commit suicide? Jack thought back to the many trials and tribulations they shared together requiring much strength and dedication to overcome. It was Ragan that charged into camp running off those two bear cubs dead set on destroying everything. It was Ragan that jumped into the freezing cold river water over his head to retrieve those three ducks that were shot down because he did not believe in wasting a life. Ragan was in the deer stand, turkey blind, duck impound first, before, after or longer than any other hunter in camp. Ragan did those things not because he was super competitive, but because plowing full steam ahead was generally how Ragan lived all of his life. His dependability and loyalty were Ragan's best features…at least they were the traits Jack liked most. The fact they spent the best part of 40 years living life harder than two good ole boys should have ever push each other was a testament to their close friendship together.

With maybe the exception of his close family, Jack knew Ragan better than anyone. They had spent many days, nights and weekends hunting, fishing and camping together. They had spent many campfires and copious amounts of questionable liquid spirits unraveling the secrets to life, love and the responsibilities that would weigh heavily on a man sometimes during the course of their lives.

Jack sat and cherished the memories of how they relied upon each other for support and comfort. Jack closed his eyes and he could recall the satisfied look on Ragan's face as he would sip bourbon and bask in the glow of potential understanding for all of the world's problems. Seemed like the more liquid courage they sipped together the clearer their understanding with the wilds and ways of hunting dogs, quail coveys, striped bass migration, children, teal season and women. (Incomplete list does not reflect order of difficulty.) They were definitely two peas in the same old wrinkled pod often contemplating the value and meaning of life.

Jack and Ragan often stood hand and hand together battling biting insects, frozen duck ponds, muddy swamp roads and rabbit briar thickets. These were not mere wasted moments in time soon to be forgotten, but meaningful times spent tempering the bond between two kindred spirits. They discovered each other's strengths and limitations and celebrated both. Their friendship was forged into a tight brotherhood that was sometimes hard for others to understand. But they knew what words could never explain.

A person's life is a precious and generous thing to share. Exposing your naked thoughts, dreams, fears and your inner soul for judgment by another person is a humbling and dignified experience. Some people may conclude that marriage is a lot like this deep level of giving of one's self to a best friend. But Jack thought marriage was structured a bit differently. Being married and having a true best friend were not the same. In a marriage, you sign up for the obligation on a special pre-planned day with a big party. Whereas a best friend has to earn your trust and respect sometimes under the most difficult of circumstances and must continue to prove their worthiness every single day within its own merit for the friendship to survive. There is no short cut or binding document to structure the relationship.

While Jack sat staring at the fire, memories of his friend and the moments they shared together occupied him completely. He could not remove Ragan from his thoughts and realized more than ever how Ragan had taken a permanent residence in his heart. The shotgun leaning in the corner of the room, the deer picture hanging on the wall, and the beat up duck decoy resting on the mantel were all painful reminders of his friend and the time they had spent together. Jack felt lost. He felt betrayed. He was beginning to get angry that his friend left him to blindly rumble down the road of life without the comfort and stability their friendship had afforded. The lonesome hurt Jack was feeling had now settled in the lower pit of his stomach. And if Jack knew nothing at all he knew this: Ragan's death would bring about a tremendous change in his life. Jack didn't want to accept what the future would be like without his loyal, trusted friend. But it was painfully evident he now had no choice in the matter.

"Well old man," Jack said out loud. "Since you are hanging out with me today, guess there is but one thing to do. We'll have a drink for ole time's sake."

Jack stood from his chair and walked over to a familiar cabinet. Jack set two tumblers on the table and without looking, reached into the cabinet and pulled out a bottle of his finest bourbon. He poured two drinks without ice anticipating the warmth that was to come from each sip. In a friendly but firm voice Jack said out loud, "hope you didn't think I was gonna drink alone?"

One by one Jack allowed every memory of his friend and their experiences together to come rushing back in great detail without resistance. Every double on ducks, every missed shot, every long hard day behind a pointer, every picture they ever took, every secret they ever shared, every heartbreaking blood trail they followed, all of their memories together came rushing back for Jack's emotional inspection.

Time flowed without notice as Jack's inventory of memories was long and satisfying. At the end of his happy reverie, Jack found himself also at the bottom of a once half full fifth of brown spirits. "Why commit suicide?" Jack said in a slow, soft, contemplative voice. It was discovered after Ragan's death that he had cancer. No one knew. Why did Ragan not tell anyone about his condition? Why the secret? Jack could understand Ragan not telling his daughters if his goal was to protect them from heartbreak. But why not tell his best friend? Same reason?

Jack was now feeling more somber than angry; he sat stoic in his chair watching the last of the embers glow in the fireplace. Jack thought about how he might react if he had terminal cancer. Mindlessly tapping his finger on the arm of the chair, Jack thought about what an ordeal Ragan must have had to face when answering the same question. What could a man of Ragan's strength and courage have been thinking to have caused him to make the decisions he made. Jack contemplated with much effort, could he ever be as strong as his friend?

There were whispers in quiet company about how people who commit suicide are weak and selfish. Jack bristled at the idea this explanation was somewhat offered as a way to explain his friend Ragan. Ragan was the strongest man Jack knew, stronger than himself even. Ragan certainly did not fit the stereotypical mold of a lost, disturbed sole contemplating the abyss of death as a cowardly escape to be selfish.

Certainly Ragan was no stranger to death. As a sportsman, he had embraced death as a natural part of life. He had obviously held death in his hands many times and debated its finality. What ethical hunter does not revere death as a real and significant part of living? Some would say that death to animals and death to humans are two different things. However, in reality, they aren't. Death is still death and in the end it's only final to the living.

Still sitting in his comfortable chair, Jack's cheeks were rosy from the bourbon and he noticed that he was warm. His heart was full of admiration for his friend and Jack began to feel more forgiving toward him. Jack sat working out his feelings and soon realized that if his friend Ragan was anything, he was an inspiration. Ragan had shown all of us that death was a natural part of life and should not be feared. It takes a brave and strong man to hold life and death in his hands and have dominion over it; especially when the life being held in your hand is your own.

Jack stood from his chair and poked at the dwindling coals in the fireplace. He reached for a picture frame from the mantel. It was an old photo of a much younger Jack and Ragan posing in a dove field. For the first time, Jack completely understood and appreciated the incredible strength and courage it must have taken for Ragan to have ended his life the way he lived it.

Honoring his friend, Jack raised his glass and his last sip of tribute into the air and toasted Ragan's memory. Jack couldn't help but chuckled out loud as he realized once again, time spent with an old friend and a little brown liquor is always time well spent.

Poor Religion

Going to church is a peculiar thing. Fifty people can attend church and hear the preacher give a sermon, and each person hear something different from the message. For the sake of argument, let's say the preacher was trying to convey an important message, and fifty different messages were heard. Could it be said that the preacher did an ineffective job delivering the message? It may be a poor reflection on Jack, but he would often get a kick out of watching people in the church get all riled up about such things.

There were other nuances that Jack noticed about people and religion which seemed to be somewhat universal. Like how women generally seemed to be more faithful and more serious about practicing religion than men; and how a person's colorful past and a dab of conscience contributed greatly to how quickly they would come around to living on the righteous side of the Bible. It also mattered how old a person was as to how much believ'n got done. This one amused Jack the most. Seemed like the closer a person gets to finding out what the promised land really looks like, the more attention is paid to following whatever righteous path they think will get them there. Believing in a life hereafter becomes important once you have started packing for the trip.

Jack did not darken the door at every church service, but he did regularly attend what he thought were the important ones. He did not know why he felt like going to some services and not others, but he did. There were many times Jack felt that going to church was hypocritical. The way Jack saw it, physically being in or out of church did not have anything to do with a person's level of believing. It amused Jack how some folks needed to be seen believing. As if having others witness your faith was somehow validation that it existed. Jack felt a person could pray to God anywhere, anytime, and be just as close to God as someone sitting in church doing the same. To Jack, faith was a personal journey whereby the effectiveness of what you believe, in the end, will not be the result of a congregational discussion about what to do with your soul.

Sitting in the next to the last pew on the right side, Jack listened to the preacher give his Christmas Eve sermon. Jack had heard this service so many times he could almost recite it by heart. Jack liked the Christmas Eve service the best because he enjoyed seeing the excitement in the children. Their eyes sparked with wonderment and anticipation. Jack was a child himself where Christmas was concerned. Even at his age, he could not remove the overgrown smile from his face during the entire month of December. Jack remembered his own childhood and how times were tough and how they grew up financially disadvantaged and did not having very much. But his mother always found a way to make Christmas special. If but for one day, little Jack did not have to worry about chores, being cold, sometimes hunger, and the social indignity that wearing pants too short for your legs can do to a child. No sir, Christmas was always a happy time filled with excitement and hope. Hoping for better, hoping for more, hoping for change, hoping for the strength to get by yet again for another year might sound like an odd Christmas ritual; but having hopes and dreams on the biggest make believe day of the year seemed like a natural thing to Jack.

And while that was a long time ago, Jack never forgot those early boyhood Christmases and how they created a unique Christmas spirit deep in his heart. Even when he was raising his own children, he worked very hard to make Christmas day the best day of the year. Like his mother, Jack had the gift of making Christmas personal. Christmas was not about material things as much as it was about spending quality time together. Jack learned early there was no gift greater than to give of one's self. Jack didn't know it, but his incredible outgoing, positive perspective about giving may have been influenced by his mother but was also borne out of the therapeutic process of dealing with his own deep scars of deprivation.

Jack's excitement level continued to climb as church service came to a close. Tomorrow was Christmas and his family would be making their annual pilgrimage to his house. He was looking forward to spending the day remembering old times and making new memories. Jack thought back to a time when his children were small and would waddle under his feet everywhere he went. And how they would tangle themselves in the lights on the tree and get lost in a sea of wrapping paper left on the floor. He especially liked how his daughters seemed to choose using him as their personal jungle gym to play with instead of the toys they had received as gifts. Those were happy memories and they made Jack's smile grow even larger.

Jack's daydreaming abruptly came to an end as he stepped outside and realized the weather had turned bad. There was snow and ice falling and the roads were already slick. "Only a fool would be out in this weather," Jack said light-heartily with a smile still on his face. The country roads weren't heavily traveled and driving could quickly become difficult to manage. Jack was in no hurry, thinking it was better to be safe than sorry; he decided to take the trip home slow and easy. Besides, he had most of tomorrow's Christmas dinner already prepared so there was no reason to hurry.

Visibility was poor. The storm, nightfall, and Jack's aging eyes made driving difficult. Jack was about three miles from his home when he saw a black spot off the shoulder of the road. He had almost passed the object by the time he noticed it. At first, Jack paid the object no attention but his foot instinctively let up off the gas and gently touched the brake. Jack came to a stop and opened the door to see what was there. He had to walk around to the rear of the truck to get a better look. He was surprised to see a man in a small black jacket walking on the shoulder of the road. The man did not seem to notice Jack and was walking as if in a distant trance. Jack noticed the man was not dressed to be out in this kind of bad weather. He looked to be about 26 years old and had on a worn-out John Deere ball cap, overalls, and a teddy bear stuffed under one arm. Jack moved closer and asked the man if he needed any help.

Not getting a response, Jack stepped forward and gently pulled at the man's arm and asked him if he could give him a ride. The man looked up and abruptly pulled away from Jack's grip as if in fear while clutching the bear with both hands. The man mumbled, not words, but sounds like those of a person hyperventilating. Jack put his hands up in the air and quickly said, "I don't want your bear son, I just want to help you. All I want to do is give you a ride."

The man looked terrified. Jack could see the man was shaking all over and was not sure if he was shaking from fear or from the wet cold. Nonetheless, Jack easily recognized that he needed help. Jack pleaded with the man calmly as if talking to a child, "Please let me help you son." Jack hustled over to the passenger's side door and opened it as a gesture of good intentions. The man still appeared upset and was looking from side to side as if trying to decide what to do. Jack again pleaded with the man to get into his truck and offered to take the man anywhere he wanted to go. Jack could tell this got the man's attention so he told him again, "If you will get into the truck, I will take you anywhere you want to go."

The man moved slowly questioning Jack's intentions, and stood at the open door. Jack ran around and climbed into the driver's side door quickly stepping on the clutch and pulling at the gearshift. The man was still standing at the open truck door contemplating whether or not he should trust Jack. Feeling cold and exasperated, Jack said, "Do you want a ride or not, this kind of weather could kill someone." The seriousness of Jack's comment struck chord with the man convincing him to take a chance on the sincerity of Jack's offer for a ride. The man climbed into the truck and shut the door.

The man urgently pointed down the road as if to give Jack directions. Jack started down the road and the man rolled down the window and stuck his head out into the wind like a dog would do on a hot summer's day in order to get a better view of where they were going. Jack slowly drove down the road while the man looked out the window and gave directions by pointing his finger.

They turned left down Four Pond Road and went about two miles when the man started making that hyperventilating sound again and insistently motioned for Jack to stop. Jack pulled to the side of the road into the driveway of an old homestead. Jack barely got the truck stopped when the man flung open the door and took off running down the overgrown drive. Instinctively, Jack followed after him. The drive led to an abandoned farmhouse that was used many years ago by transient farm workers. The house was extremely run down and had not been lived in for years. The left side of the porch roof had fallen in, glass in some of the windows had been broken out, and the siding looked faintly white-washed evidence that paint did existed on the siding at one time.

When Jack got to the steps, he could see inside through the door left open by the urgency of the man he was following. He saw a small fire in the broken down fireplace and the man holding, hugging, and clinging to a small little girl. The girl must have been about six years old. She had long blond hair that was in her face and knotted. She was dressed in a dirty red jacket with what used to be white wool on the cuffs and collar. The jacket pocket was torn. The girl was in a dress but was also wearing pants and leather shoes too big for her feet. Her shoes dangled off her heels when the man picked her up to hold her.

Jack watched as the man, now on one knee, clung to the girl moaning and mumbling. Jack was not sure if the sounds he made were happy or sad, but the girl seemed to understand. The light from the fire was low, but Jack could see the look on the little girl's face when the man presented her with the teddy bear. It was the same look Jack knew all too well, the look he liked to call "Christmas surprise". The girl was overjoyed with the teddy bear and quickly pulled it under her chin with both arms as she hugged it. She smiled back at the man with sparkles in her eyes.

The teddy bear had a red bow on its head and looked like the kind of bears being sold down at the convenience store not far from where Jack found the man on the road. Jack was not sure, but the bulge in his throat and the effort required to hold back tears told Jack that he had just witnessed the presentation of Christmas to that little girl. Judging from her joyful response as she began nuzzling her nose in the bear's brown furry belly, it was the best Christmas present ever.

Still standing at the front steps, Jack felt a rush of cold running up his pant legs. Jack was not dressed for bad weather. He immediately thought about the way the man had been dressed and the personal sacrifice he endured to go out in this awful, foul weather to get that Christmas bear for the girl.

Jack knew all too well the sting of despair. And while Jack's heart went out to that little girl, it was the man that broke Jack's heart the most. Because to really know despair also means you know the difference of living without it. The little girl was too young and appeared not to know the difference. But the man knew better, and the weight of despair heavily adorned his stature with feelings of helplessness and abandonment that despair can cause deep in a person's spirit.

Jack slowly took a few steps back and looked away from the sight that was gripping his chest and making it hard for him to breath. He had seen enough. Memories of despair from his own life were brought back to him freshly opening old wounds. Jack remembered distinctly when he first felt the sting of despair. He was a young boy at Christmas a long time ago. His mother had one wrapped gift under the tree for each of her four sons, and when the presents were opened, Jack got the best present ever, a folding pocketknife. This was a signal to young Jack that he was growing up. He also thought it was a rite of passage that a boy could not become a man until he had a pocketknife. Jack also thought about how much easier his life would be having a pocketknife to help him complete some of his chores and responsibilities around the farm. But Jack's younger brother also thought the knife was a dandy gift and wanted it for himself. Jack's brother wanted the knife so much that he was willing to trade his gift, a new pair of shoes, for the knife.

New shoes usually meant they were new to you, not necessarily new-never-been-worn shoes. These shoes were actually off the store shelf, never been worn new shoes. Jack considered how wonderful the boost in his pride would feel to have new shoes.

Young Jack was at the age where he could feel the sting of public notice for his family's poor misfortunes. Jack felt that having new shoes instead of the torn ones he was currently wearing would be one less thing he would feel self conscious about. But what really made the exchange with his brother even more important was how young Jack thought it was his responsibility to protect his brother from waking up and discovering despair no sooner than was absolutely necessary. If having that pocketknife meant his brother could remain happy-go-lucky for another little while, then making the trade was worth it to Jack. That Christmas taught Jack the difference between living innocently among desperate circumstances and living with the full weight and knowledge of despair on your shoulders.

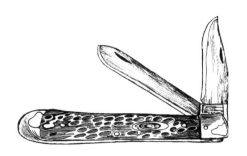

Jack took a deep breath and willed up enough courage to step back up onto the porch and into the doorway. He announced his presence by loudly clearing his throat. Startled, the man scooped the little girl into his arms and took a few steps back while looking at Jack with wild eyes of escape. He was still shaking and appeared to be sweating. Jack stepped inside and stuck out his hand toward the man and introduced himself, "Hi, my name is Jack Seavers".

Jack's uninvited hand awkwardly suspended in the air a second or two before he quickly put it back into his coat pocket. Now in better light, Jack recognized the man as a farm hand hired to work on the Dixie farm about a mile down the road. Rumor around town was that the man could not speak and was maybe a little mentally slow. Jack knew little about the man, having only seen him a time or two around town, and that people called him Buddy. Jack was not sure if Buddy was his real name, or a name given to him much like a throw away name casually given to a stray dog.

Instinctively, Jack followed up his awkward introduction by saying, "I've heard folks in town call you Buddy and I think you work on the Dixie farm". The man and the little girl stood clinging together looking at Jack as if he were a ghost. Jack made a few quick glances around the room and could tell they had been living in the run-down abandoned house for a while. There did not appear to be any food in the house. A few small tree limbs was all they had for firewood. There was no bedding of any kind and they looked to be wearing all the clothes they owned.

The man did not appear to be retarded. But he did not, or could not speak, and it concerned Jack that the man did not look well. He was still uncontrollably shivering and he look exhausted. Jack could tell the man was a good man and had a good heart by the warm, kind way he treated his daughter and how she affectionately responded back to him. The pair were inseparable and held on to each other tightly as if holding on to their only valuable possession.

And so it was, three lost souls standing in the dim glow of the feeble firelight of that old house. Looking back now, none of them would be able to fully comprehend the extent of the miracle that happened that night. Jack was drawn to them because of his unique understanding of their circumstances; and they were drawn to Jack recognizing his gentle sincerity and un-judgmental heart.

Jack was able to feed, clothe, and house the pair not only for the night, but also for the rest of their short stay in the community.

It was not the material things the pair would always remember about Jack, but the love of a man who gave them hope where there was none and revived dignity where it had nearly been stomped out and extinguished.

But it was Jack who had gained the most. Found among the ruins of an abandoned farmhouse was the gift of atonement. Jack could no longer run from his childhood and the hurtful memories of seeing his mother secretly cry. He was finally able to face his demons of shame and guilt that growing up poor had left on his heart. Jack never really blamed God for his lot in life, but he did feel strongly there was a higher power in charge and a master plan for all things. Jack never understood or appreciated such a Devine plan until that special Christmas when the power of true believing was revealed to him. Just as the birth of Christ happened in a manger, the baptism of Jack's salvation happened in a run-down farmhouse without congregational witnesses, without the preacher giving a special message, and without organized ceremony. Jack's own scars of despair and doubt were washed away by his unselfish deeds. He discovered that the power of healing and believing were not things that you sometimes think about, talk about or pray about on Sunday. True redemption and relief of your personal burdens come from the acts of kindness and service that you do for others.

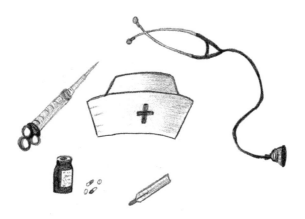

Good Medicine

It was the longest night of Jack's life. He always hated sleepless nights of tossing and turning as it usually meant he had trouble on his mind. And while he kept telling himself that it was nothing to worry about, he couldn't help feeling a little worried. Jack had been diagnosed with a serious heart condition a few months ago. Serious enough that Jack did not tell his family the entire truth about his condition. Of course, they knew there was to be more testing and that a future plan of action would eventually be needed to fix the problem. However, his family did not know surgery had already been scheduled and that it was a common but touchy procedure.

Having a stubborn disposition, Jack was not going to tell his family about the surgery or that he was going to the hospital by himself. He was just an old, simple country fellow maybe tied a little too tight to the old ways of doing things. Running around upsetting folks with your personal problems was not how Jack was raised. He knew he would be in the doghouse with his family when they found out, but for this, even Jack did not have an excuse. He did not want people to fuss over him. He had even admitted to himself that he was wrong for his bull headed decision, but that did not mean he was going to change his mind.

Jack made the hour-and-a-half drive to the hospital in his old pick-up truck. The farm truck was slow but dependable. Judging from the blank stares of the other travelers on the highway, Jack could tell his beat up farm truck was getting a lot of attention. Jack actually got a kick out of waving to the other drivers as they passed him by. He figured that since his trip to the hospital was being done "on the lamb", he might as well have a little fun with it. At least that was how he rationalized his fear of being sick.

Jack was nervous about the medical procedure. He was maybe even a little unsure about his decision not to completely inform his family about what he was doing. Overall, his main concern was generally about being sick in the first place. Jack wasn't the type of person to get sick very often and he could never really remember a time when he was ever scared about anything. His illness was serious and Jack was struggling emotionally trying to figure out a way to cope with his condition, a coping process he felt compelled to do alone.

Since the paperwork at the hospital had been pre-submitted weeks ago, all Jack had to do was show up. The hospital smelled of antiseptic. A smell he did not like. Jack told the receptionist his name and she said, "Yes Mr. Seavers, we have been expecting you." Within a few minutes, a young, smiling nurse came around the corner with a wheel chair. Seeing the chair added to Jack's anxiety and his guilt for keeping the procedure secret. Jack all of a sudden felt overwhelmed with regret and wanted to confess the sins of his stubborn behavior to his family. But before he could really say anything, the young energetic nurse said, "Mr. Seavers, I am your nurse and my name is Cindy. I am going to take you to various departments for last minute testing, then you will be put to sleep and we will operate to see if we can make you feel better."

Jack momentarily woke from a deep sleep. Even though he had been sleeping for a week, he did not feel rested. A nurse walked into the room to check on Jack and appeared happy to find him awake. It seemed to Jack that he was hooked to every kind of machine known to mankind and the beeping and buzzing noises scared him. He did not think this kind of treatment to be the aftermath of a routine procedure. He asked the nurse with an air of confidence trying to hide his deepening concerns, "How am I doing?"

The nurse responded, "Mr. Seavers, you have been a very sick man. The operation turned out to be a lot harder than anyone expected, and your recovery has been just as difficult. There were times when we had to work hard to keep you around."

The nurse's report caught Jack by surprise and he had a loss for words. He was in shock upon hearing the nurse report on his condition. Suddenly, Jack felt sick to his stomach. He was riddled with guilt and regret over having been such a selfish, old man. All he could think about was how worried his family must be not knowing where he was or what he was doing. He felt like a kid again, in trouble with his parents for having done something wrong and was now dreadfully awaiting his due punishment. Only Jack wasn't a kid anymore and this situation was far more serious than any trouble he had ever entertained as a rough-housing youngster. Of all the hardheaded stunts to pull, coming here for this procedure without letting anyone know surely signified senility, he could think of no other rational excuse.

"Mr. Seavers, you are a lucky man. You must have an angel watching over you. And if it weren't for nurse Cindy, I'm afraid you might not be with us," the nurse said.

"Nurse Cindy?" Jack questioned.

"Yes Mr. Seavers, Nurse Cindy has been by your side day and night for the last week and the doctor finally made her go home to get some rest. She agreed only after I said I would watch after you until her return. She should be back in a couple of hours. Is Cindy a relative?" asked the nurse.

"No… I don't think I know the young lady, but I am grateful from the bottom of my heart to have been in her care," Jack added thoughtfully. "This sure is a special hospital to give patients this kind of personal treatment."

"Mr. Seavers, Cindy took vacation time in order to take care of you and you only. That is why I asked if she was a relative. There wasn't a time when she wasn't holding your hand or stroking you gently on the head. It took a whole week, but I think she told you her entire life's story in great detail," the nurse told Jack.

As the nurse was leaving to inform the doctor of Jack's waking, the door to his room frantically flung opened and his daughter came rushing inside. She ran to his side and through her tears, kissed him on the cheek and wrapped her arms around his neck. Underneath her sobbing breaths, Jack's daughter kept repeating the only words that would come out, "Daddy- Daddy- Daddy," over and over again. Jack never intended to hurt anyone. His intentions not to burden anyone with his problems were honorable at the time. How was he to know that a simple in-and-out routine procedure would turn into an actual threat to his life?

"Daddy, we have all been so worried about you. We didn't know where you were or what had happened to you. The entire family has been trying to find you for days," his daughter informed him.

"Honey, I am so sorry to have troubled you. It was never my intention to hide anything from you. You know how I hate to bother other people with my problems and I really did not think this procedure would have turned out to be such a big ordeal," Jack said with a genuine voice of regret and concern.

"Daddy, you are very important to us. It seems that lately the more we tell you how much we care the more you push us away. Why Daddy, why do you push us away?" asked his daughter still holding on to his neck with both arms.

Jack thought for a minute before answering, and while he did not feel comfortable talking about the issue, he did not think he could avoid the question. His guilt for what he had put his family through was overwhelming and he felt that at the very least he owed his daughter an explanation. Jack spoke in that tender voice usually reserved for his grandchildren when he was about to explain a life lesson. Jack said, "You know, it is hard to admit when you aren't the man you used to be. In some ways, it is embarrassing to let your family, who has always counted on you to be a pillar of strength, see you become weak and fragile. It is hard to keep your dignity when you can see and feel Father Time squeeze the life right out of you. It's hard for you to understand, but some day you will be where I am and will know the truth of what I speak."

His daughter did understand, but instead of being angry with her father, she felt guilty she had not done a good enough job showing or convincing her father how important he was to her. "Daddy, I remember when me and my sister were little; you would throw us into the air and catch us in your strong arms. You would let us ride on your back until your knees hurt. You would swing us and you were always there to kiss our boo boos. Daddy, I don't want to swing anymore or ride on your back. What I need from you now is to be there for me. I need the security of knowing that the greatest man in the world is beside me giving me strength when I'm not sure I can make it through another hectic day. I need your hugs of reassurance. And now that I have grown up, I have a need and desire deep inside me to take care of you. I need to show you how much I love you. Daddy, you have got to be man enough to let people love you, do for you, wait on you if they want, and be there for you. Just like you took pride in being a good father to me, don't take away my opportunity to be a good daughter to you."

Jack understood completely, and while it was never discussed again, he could feel the power dynamic in their relationship shift from him to his daughter. He now felt for the first time that he held a subservient role in their relationship. This was a new and odd feeling for Jack that would take some time getting used to. But for the moment, Jack was relieved to be in his daughter's company and he felt much comfort having her with him.

"Daddy, where did the beautiful flowers come from?" his daughter asked. Without Jack saying a word, she went over and took the card that was taped to the vase. "Daddy, it's a letter. Do you want me to open it? Do you want me to read it to you?" Jack nodded and his daughter opened the envelope and inside was a beautiful get well card and a hand written letter of many pages that said:

Dear Jack,

I thought I recognized you the moment I saw you, and when I heard your voice it lingered with me for a long time as something familiar and wonderful. It wasn't until I later saw your address on your admittance papers that I knew who you were. Even though, I don't believe you know who I am. For this, I am truly sorry that I have allowed many years to pass without contacting you. You will never know how much your love and kindness have influenced my life. Because of you, I have become a nurse and have dedicated myself to helping others.

I will always be in debt to you for saving my father and I from that run-down farmhouse where you found us so many years ago. The job you helped my father get on that horse farm was the best job he ever had. My father happily worked there until his premature death a few years ago. The lady of that farm took me under her wing as a child and made sure that I went to school and had every opportunity to make something of myself. Because of you, I did not have to live dirty, cold, hungry or ashamed. My father was able to work for good people that did not take advantage of him or make fun of his mental handicap. Because of you, I realized what it means to have blessings and angels watching over me. You were my angel Jack. Your spirit has lived within me and guided me during times when I have felt lost.

Words cannot express my gratitude or the prominent place you hold in my heart. You gave me the strength to believe in dignity, you let me know I deserved happiness, you gave me reasons to have hope, and the pride to never be put down or held down by anyone. Jack, you gave me the world.

It is difficult to sit beside you and watch as you fight for your life. It hurts me to think that I may never have the chance to thank you in person for being the wonderful man that you are. My father never forgot you and your kindness, and he took to his grave your memory and the proud dignity you created within him on that Christmas Eve so long ago.

And while you lie here before me in what others might see as a fragile state, I see courage and bravery of a strong man. I will do everything in my power to see that you recover completely from this operation and have many more years of life to live. I know this sounds selfish, but I need you to live. I need to see you and talk to you. I need to show you my success and thank you for lighting the fire that revived my limp, lifeless body and spirit. I need to show you what a savior looks like because I will always and forever be ...... your little farm girl,

Cindy

Tears welled in Jack's eyes as his daughter read the note. There was not a day that went by when Jack did not think about Buddy and the little girl. Jack was saddened to learn Buddy had died. Neither did Jack previously realize the little farm girl named Cindy was also nurse Cindy. Jack reached for a tissue sitting on the bedside table for his watering eyes. As he did so, he noticed a pile of neatly folded blankets and a pillow sitting on the love seat near the window. On top of the pillow was a well used brown teddy bear with a red bow on its head. It was the same teddy bear Jack remembered from that special Christmas in the old farmhouse so many years ago.

Seeing the bear made Jack remember the pocketknife he had given his brother when they were kids. It was apparent the bear had provided as much comfort to Cindy as the knife did for his brother as Jack remembered how his brother still carried the knife in his pocket everyday.

The knife and bear had become symbols of hope and inspiration and were considered treasured possessions because of the tremendous love and sacrificial spirit in which they had been given.

"Daddy, it was nurse Cindy that called me a few hours ago telling me you were here and how you were doing. I don't know how she found me or my phone number, but she was very concerned and seemed to have been crying on the phone. Is this the same little girl that stayed with you for a few weeks that time at Christmas?" his daughter questioned.

Jack did not answer his daughter's question. He stared at the bear and remembered the little girl, how she was shy and quiet, and how she and her father cowered and flinched at times. Behavior he had often seen in dogs when harshly overcorrected too many times by their master. He remembered her knotted blond hair; her skinny little arms and legs. It made Jack sad to remember. But Jack also remembered her cute and energetic smile that would pop out when she thought no one was watching, and how she was full of child-like curiosity and innocence.

Jack never wanted to hurt anyone or cause anyone trouble on his account. He always figured his mission in life was to help others. And while he did not feel as though he had very much to contribute to society anymore, he realized that he could indeed still touch people's lives by helping them realize and tend to their own emotional needs and broken spirits. Jack now realized that by allowing others to help him, he was allowing them to heal and fill empty spaces within themselves. Jack had learned a lesson long ago in that old run-down farmhouse that "believing" in something meant "doing something about it." Only now, Jack understood that "doing" was not only good for his soul, but "doing" was also good medicine for others.

> Author's Note: I have no desire to write a novel. I only want to write stand alone, individual short stories. The only two stories that share a connection is *Poor Religion* and *Good Medicine*. I would have written this caveat earlier but I did not want to spoil your surprise when you realized for the first time the link between the two stories. Hope you were surprised.

In The Life of Jack

In the life of Jack, every day was precious and lived with joy and gratefulness. Jack had a firm sense of optimistic energy for the unknown surprises and challenges that would often accompany each new day. At times, some days were harder than others to understand. The adventure of living every day to its fullest extent was always exciting to Jack. There are many people who would say that Jack lives a simple life. Jack himself believed he indeed was a simple man. But that still did not negate the fact that around the corner of each new day was an adventure waiting to be discovered. Jack refused to live any other way.

This day was shaping up to be another glorious day. Jack had started the morning early, like always. He tended to the morning chores around the farm, as was his routine. Breakfast was now behind him including washing the dishes, the tidy kitchen made him smile. It was late September and Jack was sitting in the front porch swing enjoying a warm mid-morning respite. There was an unsteady, cool breeze that gently puffed across his face. Fall was returning once again and he could feel the anticipation in his bones.

Jack sat casually shuffling his feet causing the swing to slowly rock back and forth. He was not necessarily thinking about anything in particular but he was excited about the coming of autumn. He sat reminiscing about the smell of smoke from a warm fire. He could almost taste the apple pie from the fruit that would soon ripen to perfection and fall to the ground. And Jack could almost feel the dirt under his finger nails thinking about how he would soon dig sweet potatoes from the garden. The culinary possibilities he would make with them had Jack's appetite growing with new vigor. Jack noticed leaves on the trees were starting to turn colors and he smiled to himself thinking how fall was truly a magical season.

As Jack sat aimlessly rocking in the swing, he soon had an idea for a walk. It had been about two weeks since Jack last checked his mailbox posted up on the main highway. He was sure the mailman was probably tired by now of having to stuff junk mail into an already over-filled box.

Jack sprang from the swing with purpose to retrieve a paper sack with handles that would assist him with purging the box. He was confident the paper sack was large enough to sufficiently hold all the junk mail he expected to find. Out the front door, off the porch and down the long drive Jack walked keeping a brisk pace. He felt energized and a little smile curled at the ends of his lips accenting his happy expression while he enjoyed the exercise.

Jack began to laugh out loud as he approached the mail box seeing the door would hardly closed with all the junk mail hanging out around the sides. He opened the mailbox door all the way exposing what he had already suspected…. Yep, an over flow of junk mail. Jack pulled at the mound of brightly colored paper skillfully printed to catch the attention of would be consumers. Advertising circulars from grocery stores, car dealerships, fast food restaurants and from various lending institutions guaranteeing Jack a loan of questionable amounts of money made up the bulk of the load. There were a few church fliers advertising their Sunday morning worship and Sunday school hours with an encouraging invitation to attend. Jack rarely received what he considered "real" mail anymore. Friends and family knew how to pick up the phone and call if he was needed. No one wrote letters anymore and the act of staying in touch by mail was becoming a lost art. That's why the pale blue envelope was so strikingly out of place.

With much curiosity, Jack turned the envelope over so he could see the front side. The envelope looked to be the size and shape one would expect with a greeting card. He thought quickly about who might be getting married or having a baby as he usually received social invitations of that kind. But as the card turned and the light hit the front of the envelope illuminating his name, Jack had to catch his breath. Actually, Jack stopped breathing altogether and an uncontrollable hiccup of surprise escaped from the back of his throat. He dropped the junk mail sack to the ground and held the envelope with both hands. Jack looked away for a second trying to settle the hundreds of swirling thoughts now competing for his attention. He glanced back at the handwriting on the front. His smile disappeared and Jack was nervously trying to rescue his heart that seemed to have stopped beating.

With a herculean effort to regain his composure, Jack took a huff of air into his lungs and blinked for the first time since seeing the letter. He stared at the handwriting with dis-belief. His face felt flush. Overwhelming emotions were building in his chest and welling in his throat. He swallowed hard trying to hold down what he could not seem to control. His eyes felt damp as he clutched the envelope a little tighter as if securing its safety was suddenly important.

A light breeze across the envelope brought a familiar scent to Jack's nose and he breathed deeply taking in the aroma. A tear fell from his cheek onto the pale blue paper turning the wet spot on the envelope a darker shade of blue. Jack held the envelope close to his chest with one hand as he wiped his eyes with the back of his other. Again, he looked at his name and the penmanship hoping it had somehow change into something different since the last time he read it. There was no doubt the handwriting was real and the envelope felt heavy in his hands. There was no return address on the envelope but Jack knew. He could never forget…. Even though there had been times when he wished he could.

Jack grabbed the bag of junk mail and hurried up the shade covered driveway back to his house. He was out of breath when he reached the front porch. Sitting the junk mail sack by the front door, Jack took a seat in the swing once again. He had now regained control of his emotions and sat holding the letter in his lap. He was thankful there were no witnesses to his earlier emotional outburst and he felt a little childish and embarrassed for having reacted the way he did. The letter was such an un-expected surprise that it caught Jack completely off guard. He was not immediately prepared to face the wealth of emotions the letter stirred within him.

Jack lifted the envelope to his nose once again. The smell was unmistakable. It was her. It was Jack's first true love and she smelled wonderful. She smelled sixteen again and Jack started to remember the first time he ever saw her....

She was a new transfer student at Jack's High School. On her first day she managed to capture the attention of every boy breathing or having a pulse. She was willowy tall with long arms. Her cheek bones were pronounced and positioned high above her chin. Her cheeks were thin but they had shown the promise of dimples when she smiled. She had a perfect nose that came to a delicate sharp point. Her lips were thin and washed with a natural red color. Her hair was cut to include arched shaped bangs and her hair was parted down the middle. Her straight, long sandy colored locks of hair hung down a little past her shoulders. She was beautiful and Jack remembered being smitten with her from the very beginning.

Her name was Sam. Sam was short for Samantha. While the name Sam for a girl would invite one to think she may have been somewhat of a tomboy, nothing could have been further from the truth. Sam was all girl. Thinking back, fondly remembering her, Jack recalled her having narrow hips and a thin frame. Her shoulders were small but gracefully carried her long neck. Sam's body style was evenly, cultishly proportioned. It was clear that Sam still had not completely finished filling out what Mother Nature had planned.

Jack sat in the swing feeling humbled as he remembered her. She captured the attention of the entire school but it was Jack that won her attention. He remembered the first time she noticed him......

Sam had been at school maybe three weeks. She still had not made many friends. Jack was sitting alone in the cafeteria at lunch when Sam took a seat directly across from him. Jack looked up from the book he was reading and expressed a bashful smile as he looked into the most amazing hazel gray eyes he had ever seen. "Hi, my name is Sam," she said.

Sam's abrupt presence and warm greeting caught Jack by surprise. He was slow to respond and appeared to be tongue tied for words. When Jack did speak, what he finally said came out as a low mumble of something not even he understood. As if to have sympathy upon his calamity, the most angelic voice Jack had ever heard quickly said, "Jack, do you mind if I sit with you?"

"Sure, I don't mind at all." Jack nervously assured her.

Jack had been aware for some-time now how his extreme country upbringing sometimes put him in uncomfortable social settings where he did not always know how to appropriately respond. This was one of those times. He was unsure if he should go back to reading his book or try to have a conversation with Sam. And if he tried to have a conversation... what

would he say? Thankfully, Sam spoke first, "Jack, I am having trouble with advanced math. I noticed you are in my class and appear to do well with the subject. We also have the same study hall, would you mind showing me what I am doing wrong?"

Jack was surprised she was asking HIM for assistance and responded, "Sure, I would be glad to do what I can to help." Jack was aware of words coming out of his mouth but they sounded as if they were an echo coming from some far-away place. Sam smiled at Jack and he was momentarily stunned by the radiance of her happy glow.

Jack sat slowly pushing the swing with his foot as he remembered how they spent the entire lunch break talking; but for the life of him could not recall what their conversation was about. He recalled how it did not take long for him to become comfortable around Sam. As the weeks past, they began spending more and more time together. Jack helped her with advanced math in study hall and she sat with him most days at lunch. Jack recalled the moment he became truly aware of their special friendship….

It was again during lunch when Sam leaned over the table toward Jack and used a whispering voice to ask, "Jack, why does everyone seem to hate me?"

Jack was surprised by her question and he thought carefully before responding. "Sam, I don't think anyone hates you. I have not heard a cross word about you from anyone. However, I must tell you that most of the boys are too bashful to talk to you because you are outgoing and pretty, and the girls are somewhat jealous of you for about the same reasons."

Sam's face and neck became flush with extra color. Her bottom lip quivered and she looked as if she were about to cry. Exposing her inner most secrets of insecurity to Jack, Sam said solemnly, hesitantly fearing his rejection of her, "Jack, I am not pretty. I hate my long skinny legs and arms. I hate my nose because I think it is too small. And small does not even start to express my dissatisfaction with my breast and butt. How, how could anyone consider me attractive?"

Jack was a simple country boy maybe not polished in the art of being a social butterfly. But his honesty and sincerity had no equal. He reached across the empty space between them and put his hand over Sam's hand that was nervously resting on the table. Jack simply said, "I think you are an amazing person and perhaps the prettiest girl I have ever seen." Looking deep into her eyes he saw her naïve, worried soul looking back. Jack realized at that moment how utterly clueless Sam was about her beauty and about how close to the surface she held her insecurities. He quickly admired her humble nature. Jack realized that she had opened up to him and trusted him to confide her innermost doubts and fears. Jack said in a soft, reassuring tone, "I will be your friend, if you want me to? You can trust me." Sam gave Jack a bashful smile and he could see happiness wash over her mood once again.

The porch swing was now standing still as Jack sat bent over with his elbows on his knees and his face in his hands remembering his youth with careful reservations. His memories were concise and clear as though Jack were actually reliving those precious moments with Sam all over again. Not surprising, his feelings and emotions were just as vivid as the day they were created. Jack thought about previous remembrances of Sam over the years and the searing pain of longing for her that always followed. This was the first time, in a long time, that Jack allowed himself to remember her freely. He was aware of the dangerous game he was playing with his heart but was willing to chance that he could control his feelings… at least he was going to try. Jack did not want to think of the painful consequences should he fail.

Instead, Jack continued to fondly remember Sam and how their friendship blossomed. Even though Jack introduced Sam to many new friends, it was always Jack with whom she chose to spend her time. She trusted Jack. He had proven himself to be the most loyal and supportive friend she had ever had.

Jack too relaxed more and more around Sam as their friendship continued to flourish. Jack soon came to know her better than anyone. He admired her quick wit, her genuine personality, her open nature of being herself without apology, and her fierce loyalty to friends and family were truly inspiring. She gave all of herself: her heart, her soul and her spirit unconditionally to people whom she loved. And she chose the people she allowed to get close to her wisely.

Without concern for the longing that was building within his heart, Jack's memories transported him back in time once again. Jack was completely consumed in reverie as he remembered the first time she told him she loved him…

Their junior year of high school had come to an end and summer was just beginning. Jack invited Sam to spend the day at the lake. It was the first Saturday of June and it would turn out to be a day neither of them would soon forget. They had been to the lake a few times before with friends but never by themselves as a date. He picked her up from her house. She had prepared a picnic basket and he had packed a cooler with ice and soft drinks. He distinctly remembered how the white sandy beach was warm under their beach towels. They spent the day throwing Frisbee, swimming, rafting and playing video games at the arcade. It was the most comfortable friendship either of them had ever experience. Their time together was effortless. After spending the day with much laughter and good natured banter, they were surprised and a bit disappointed when the sun began to set. Sam pulled Jack down to sit with her on the beach as they watched the sparkling rays of the setting sun shimmer on the water. She snuggled under his arm and he wrapped her in his embrace. Already six feet tall, Jack rested his chin on the top of her head while she nuzzled her head against his chest. No words were being spoken and the silence was appropriate. It was a timeless moment. After a short while, Sam pulled her head away from his chest and looked up into his adoring eyes. Their lips naturally came together with a soft embrace. Sam pulled back just a little and made eye contact with him again and simply whispered, "I love you Jack."

Jack was jolted back to reality as he became aware of the heavy feelings and fresh emotions that were settling in the pit of his stomach. The pain he feared came fast and hard clutched around his heart and he openly wept. It was the first real love for them both. He remembered how much they meant to each other and how she was his everything.

Jack was feeling uncomfortable. He stood from the swing and paced up and down the length of the porch. He absentmindedly rubbed the back of his neck to relieve building stress. He felt their love welling up within him just as strong as it had ever been. His breathing was short and labored. His mouth was dry. His gut physically hurt and his heart was longing for her and what once was between them.

Jack had lived a long and satisfying life. He struggled every day to make sense of the world around him. He had come to understand there were many things: experiences, opportunities, people and yes, even love that could not be explained. He considered young love to be one of those hard to explain concepts. It is a commonly held belief by adults that young "teen" love is only a simple, irrelevant case of puppy love. That until a person becomes a mature "adult" would love ever have any real significant meaning. Jack thought differently. Jack was certain that PURE LOVE could only exist as young love. It is the type of love that is seeded and nurtured in a virgin heart unsoiled by past prejudices; a love that is allowed to grow strong and true unencumbered by adult responsibilities and circumstances.

Young love is unique in that it happens at a time in a person's life when things like trust and forever are still naive concepts. When giving yourself completely to another person without reservation feels natural without guarded concern. Jack was living proof that young love was indeed real and even more everlasting.

Jack looked up and noticed the un-opened letter sitting on the porch swing. He thought maybe it had caused enough trouble for one day. He sat picking up the letter agonizing over what he should do with it. One way or the other, resolve for his pain would never come until he opened the letter. He might as well deal with it now.

Jack's fingers gently pried under the closed flap of the envelope and with a tug the flap opened. He reached in and pulled out a hand written letter on beautiful floral stationary. When he opened the letter he easily recognized her handwriting and her perfume filled his nostrils reminding him of her essence. A tear quickly ran down his cheek dropping onto the letter causing the ink to run. Wiping the clouds from his eyes with his shirt sleeve, Jack began to read the letter:

My Dearest Jack,

I hope this letter finds you safe and sound. If I know you, this letter will find you on the farm living in harmony. I think of you every day. I am actually sorry that it has taken me so long to write this letter. Thoughts of you… of us, and of what we shared together are hard to control sometimes. Please excuse the child like hope I still have for us that refuses to die within me. I get distracted sometimes wondering. It is almost impossible to convince my heart that what we once shared can never exist again.

As for the purpose of this letter, I think it is fair to say that I hated you for a long time; breaking up with me after high school graduation was devastating. I heard you say that our love could never last between us… how you were going to work on the farm and how you pushed me to pursue my dream in dance where I ultimately gained national fame and had a long and fulfilling career.

Looking back, I did not see your wisdom when you tried to explain to me how my inner fire was not on a farm and how your inner light would quickly extinguish in a city. It took me a long time to realize the value of what you did for me.... and for us. I have since come to understand the true depth of your unselfish love to push me away in order to preserve my ultimate happiness. I have always admired your strength and courage and have often used your selfless example to guide me along the way. I just wanted you to know that it has always been your love that has sustained me. It was your love that gave me the strength I needed to believe in myself and live life to the fullest. I realize how your unselfish sacrifice to push me forward would have been wasted had I not fulfilled my dreams. I did and...THANK YOU! I will forever be grateful.

I understand the same dynamics that made us live separate lives way back then when we were young still have not changed. You cannot live in the city and I cannot live on the farm. Our worlds are too different.... maybe now more than ever. But there are times when I still feel our hearts beating as one.

Jack, I love you. I have always loved you. And I will love you until our glow in the setting sun fades away for the last time.

Please know that you are very special to me. You were and will always be my first true love.

Yours truly and forever,

Sam

Jack nodded in agreement as he realized that Sam's love for him was still as meaningful as he held for her. He wiped his wet face with his shirt sleeve once again and stared at the letter that was now sufficiently tattered with running ink. He was happy. Jack realized he was indeed blessed to have shared his love, his heart, his very soul in a way that few people would ever experience. He loved Sam. He would always love Sam. She was his first true love and his heart would never let him forget it.

There was no return address. For that he was grateful. In that moment, Jack was not sure if he could have stayed away from her if only for a moment. The lack of a return address was a sign to Jack that maybe it was time for him to relying upon Sam's strength and wisdom to preserve the rest of their delicate future. A future of longing but knowing it could never be. Jack put the letter into the bag holding all the other junk mail then respectfully disposed of it in the trash. He didn't know why, but he suddenly felt the urge to go for a swim at the lake. He felt better knowing he could wrap himself in the memory of their time spent together on that warm, white sandy beach so long ago. In some small but symbolic way… he could be with her again.

Prayer Meetings

"Jack, you damn fool, we ain't never gonna get this old tractor running," Joe said with his typical gruff voice and negative attitude. "Joe, if you would work instead of complain, we would have had it running by now," Jack reminded him. And so their banter continued back and forth like an old, contemptuous married couple.

Joe was the son of a preacher man- God rests his soul. And like the stereotypical offspring of a preacher, Joe lived his life raising as much hell as he thought God would tolerate and still let him into heaven. Having religion forced upon him during most of his formative years, Joe thought he knew enough about the Bible and religion to know where the heaven/hell line of acceptable bad behavior was drawn. And so Joe burned hell from both ends when he was a younger man. However, this kind of rough and tumble life style left a mark on olc Joe. Turned him into a curmudgeon in his later years: a grouchy, old codger not many people would tolerate.

Jack, meanwhile, did not seem to mind his friend Joe and the biting contempt always present and accounted for in his personality. He knew Joe's rough exterior was only a cover for the good that existed within, even if Jack could not really give an example of one good deed Joe ever did without being asked. But you could always count on Joe if you needed him. And if you could stand Joe's brash straight talk peppered with a little profanity, he really was quite good working with his hands.

"Jack, when you gonna tear down this old barn and build a nice new metal building?" Joe asked.

To which Jack replied, "Don't know Joe, what is wrong with this one."

"Well Jack," Joe retorted, "Do you need me to paint you a damn picture? For starters, the thing is old and run down. The tin on the roof is about to rust through, the boards on the walls have curled up at the ends and no longer fit tight, there has never been anything but a dirt floor, and there isn't a window in the whole damn place."

Jack didn't even look up after Joe's biting remarks. He simply responded, "To answer your question Joe, I'm never getting rid of this barn. The tin and siding have that aged looked young folks are paying high dollar for in town, the dirt floor never needs cleaning, and windows cut down on the amount of wall space I use to hang my tools. Besides, if getting rid of old things for the sake of their age were a common practice; you and me both would have been put down long ago."

The barn sat on Jack's property at the edge of the pasture and served many purposes. Besides being well ventilated by the gaps in the weathered siding, it also housed farm equipment, served as the butchery during hunting season and hog killing time, was storage for hay and grain, was adorned with deer antlers and turkey fans, and most importantly, was the regular place for what the men called their "prayer meetings".

There must be some law of nature that men have a place to hangout. This place is usually not spoken about in mixed company. Matter of fact, the first unwritten law of having such a man-meeting place is that no one, especially the women folk, should never find out about it, at least not on purpose. There are times when a man does not want to be found... until he wants to be.

And while that is the intention, the reality is that most folks, including the women, usually do know about those man-meeting places and are smart enough not to allow the men to know they have caught on. Truth be known, women don't mind these man-meeting places as long as that place isn't inside the house. Which begs to ask the question, why don't men have a place inside the house? Why is a man's clandestine meeting place with his buddies usually outside? Evidence here suggests a conspiracy. Evidence also suggests men may be universally snookered from the start by the opposite side. Women naturally have an unfair advantage when it comes to claiming dominion over the inside of the house. Women are crafty at manipulating their power against all outside enemy forces that could upset the tranquil organization perceived to be important by her majesty herself when it comes to inside the house.

Whatever the case, Jack and his buddies didn't mind the barn.

At least in the barn there was no telephone, no TV, no clocks clanging around advertising the time, and no women or children getting into your business. Besides, a lot of work got done in the barn. Just the word work, automatically sends the children running. And any mention of old, hot, or dirty and the women don't want any part of it. So, the barn turned out to be the perfect place for male congregation and fellowship.

It's funny how men don't really talk all that much in unfamiliar company about their feelings and emotions. But if you have an accepting atmosphere, a place where men can hangout comfortably without fear of ridicule and unfounded judgment, men have quite a lot to say about their feelings. The right place is usually a spot whereby men won't be overheard by folks not having membership to their "inner circle". Men can sometimes express themselves with colorful language or have a tendency to talk about controversial subjects not suitable for women, children, and folks of unknown religious and political pedigree. So, if a man is going to let-it-all-hang-out, not being overheard is important, especially if he aims to stretch the truth a little and not be called down for it.

The right meeting place also includes having something to do. This is important because men don't usually look each other dead in the eye when they are talking. Having busy work to go with the conversation means you have a reason not to be looking directly at the other person. Besides, in a man's world, looking at another man dead in the eye usually means you want to fight him.

Women don't get this lack of eye contact thing. Ever notice two women talking? They literally cannot speak to each other, not even one full sentence, without looking, almost staring each other in the eyes. No wonder men and women have trouble communicating. It's like mixing oil and water.

What man has not heard these words from his significant other, "Are YOU listening to me? What did I just say? Don't turn away when I'm talking! Are YOU paying attention? And finally, women will usually follow up these accusations by, "Will you LOOK at me when I'm talking to you!" Think about it, the root of all this hen peck'n fuss has one common cause... the lack of eye contact. Face it, men and women are different... just don't let her find out about you knowing it.

Not wanting to be discovered is another important ingredient to having a good man meeting place. It also doesn't hurt if the meeting place is terribly inconvenient to access. People wanting your attention would rather wait for you to come up for air than to risk the effort and adventure to actually find you. A man needs a good quiet place to think and get away from everyday responsibilities. Most men wake every day to the nag-nag-nag of expectations by others. At the very least, what man does not have a honey-do-list tacked to the refrigerator? Please step forward anyone who has ever witnessed a woman who has a written down, pencil at the ready for check-off, honest-to-goodness, tacked-to-the-refrigerator, honey-do-list that she didn't put up herself?

There is a skillfully promoted perception that if men weren't a little on the lazy side, a honey-do-list would not be necessary. This attitude is propaganda professionally perpetrated by the enemy. Truth is, what men really think are important task to complete ranks low when compared to the official "prioritized list" of things to do prominently hung on the refrigerator by the little general. So yes, it is a challenge for a man to work up enough enthusiasm and mental muster to complete assigned task that he doesn't feel are very important in the first place.

And what self-respecting man has not learned long ago not to complain about the list or say anything stupid like: "If you want it done right now, do it yourself." Something about a woman having the "memory of an elephant" and "hell have no fury" that keeps men motivated to quietly work on the list of contrived chores that seem to grow larger and faster than the national deficit. What would it hurt if men actually got to the bottom of the list every once in a while? Or would that kind of hope and encouragement give them an unnecessary false sense of independence?

Within the confines of a "prayer meeting" a man can expose himself. I'm not talking about discretely stepping off to the side of the barn and relieve his bladder when the urge hits him. Exposing himself in this example means that he can hem-haw around and talk about what is on his mind, what may be troubling him, or how he feels about a situation, even if it makes him sad or emotional to do so.

Why a man feels comfortable opening his dark side to a select few bosom buddies and not his wife or pastor is probably due to societal expectations that a man must be strong and stable at all times. There is nothing stable or attractive about a blubbering man complaining about his problems. That kind of behavior won't get him voted in as church deacon, or will convince his wife to have his children. Society expects a man to act like he knows what he is doing, and be strong and dependable doing it.

Prayer Meetings | 97

After much banging and clanging on the tractor, Jack finally got around to asking his friend, "Hey Joe, what did the doctor say about that leaking faucet problem you had?"

Jack could tell his inquiry knocked the wind out of ole Joe. Joe became very quiet and distracted. Both men continued their busy work without a word being spoken for a long time. Finally, the silence was broken when Joe cleared his throat a couple of times. Jack could tell he wanted to say something but the words would not come out. Joe opened his mouth as if he was going to speak, but the words never came. Jack reached across the engine and patted Joe on the shoulder. Joe bowed his head and stared at the ground.

Without looking up, Joe said, "Jack, I don't have much longer to live. The doc said my problem went undetected too long, spread to other parts of my body, and has now caused serious problems in other places."

Upon hearing Joe's confession, Jack stopped what he was doing and stared at Joe who was still looking at the ground. Trying to bring stability to an uncomfortable situation, Jack asked in a stern, straightforward manner without emotion, "Have you told anyone yet?" Joe looked up at Jack and their eyes met. Voices could be disguised void of feeling, but the look in their eyes told the true story of the emotional burden each man was carrying at that moment.

"No Jack, I haven't been able to find the time, the words, or the strength to face my family with this news. Jack, I feel as though I have let them down."

Joe's reasons suspended in the air like the stench of salt-water marsh mud at low tide. Jack needed no further explanation as he knew exactly what Joe meant. It is sometimes a heavy burden to be a man; to always be strong and dependable, to be everything to everyone and then spend a lifetime ignoring your own needs and desires in an effort to fulfill that almost impossible expectation of "manhood" that society places on a boy at birth. It becomes easy, after a while, for a man to feel overwhelmed as though he is not worthy of having attention paid to himself or the plights he may encounter during the course of his life. His life can be a lonesome existence, as though a man's needs are an unnecessary burden to the rest of society.

Unfortunately, this social expectation of "manhood" is true even when his weaknesses are highlighted as a result of immortality. And while no man should ever die alone, he should not also die shackled to the unrealistic expectations of being something other than human.

Jack walked over and put his hand on Joe's shoulder and gave a gentle squeeze. "Joe, you know what you have to do," Jack said.

Without hesitation, Joe put the wrench being held in his hand down on the tractor fender and turned to Jack with a strained smile and said, "I sure am going to miss this old barn. It has meant the world to me over the years. I can't remember a time when there was someplace else I would have rather been."

Joe turned to leave and Jack called out to him adding the one and only thing he knew to say. The same words they had shared with each other for so many years. The only words that ever really meant anything to their friendship. The words that had always given them comfort, support, and had been the secret to each man successfully fulfilling the man-card given to them by way of society expectation at birth. Jack said, "Joe, if you should need me for anything, you know I am here for you. You know you don't have to face this alone." Joe looked at Jack and felt a sense of relief and he felt at peace. He knew Jack meant what he said and would indeed be there for Joe during this difficult moment just as Jack had been a dependable rock for all the difficult moments in his life.

Both men realized, while it is commonly expected that a man be a man for the rest of the world, it is sometimes more important that he be a man to other men.

And She Was

The first thing Jack noticed about her was her boots. Jack always thought you can tell a lot about a person from their shoes. She had on a pair of old work boots that were damn near worn out. They were worn down almost to the point of needing to be resoled. The leather uppers were discolored beyond any recognition of what the original color used to be. The combination of mud and manure caked to the sides left nothing to the imagination as to her profession. She was a farm girl no doubt about it. From the looks of her boots, she was not just a city girl doing the weekend farmer routine. Oh no, these boots had been doing real farming work and had been doing it for a long time.

Jack also noticed how slender she was. Most folks would have called her skinny, but Jack knew better. Skinny was a reference made about someone born with a thin frame. Being slender however, was a reference for a muscular build worn down by long hours on your feet and hard work. Her frame was solid and she walked straight as a board, tall with confidence.

It was not unusual to see a new person walking around in the Feed and Seed Store. The store had transitioned over the years to be more user friendly to the non-farming community. The store not only still carried all of the typical farm gear like garden seed, livestock feed, tack, nuts and bolts, and equipment parts; but now the store also had a large selection of yard flags, mail box covers, bird feeders, door mats and other home décor items. It was not uncommon anymore to see women in the Feed and Seed Store on a regular basis. Even so, Jack had not seen this woman before and the way she perused the store made her stand out. She looked carefully taking a genuine interest at everything in the store not just the latest in decorative gourd seeds. But what caught Jack's attention about this woman the most was how she was especially taking her time evaluating fencing options instead of night light covers. Apparently, there was a fencing project on her mind and she was giving the chore a real thoughtful workout.

It's not every day that a woman comes into the Feed and Seed Store dressed like she naturally belonged in the back woods country setting while also looking like a Paris runway model. Runway modeling and dirt farming were not synonymous concepts, nowhere remotely close to each other on the occupational scale. She was definitely a noticeable sight to say the least. Suddenly, Jack felt conscientious and sheepishly guilty for staring. It was out of character for Jack to pay so much attention to someone even if she did stick out like a black speckled pig in a litter of white piglets.

Jack felt embarrassment for his behavior so he quickly wandered over to the counter where he placed his order for chicken feed and dog food. Facing the clerk with his back to the sales floor, Jack could follow the woman's movements around the store by watching the clerk's eyes as they darted in her direction with quick, and hopefully, unnoticed glances. This relieved Jack of his guilt as he realized that he was not the only person that found the young lady note-worthy.

Loading receipt in hand, Jack made his way to his truck and drove around to the rear of the building where there was a loading dock. This is where Jack would wait while a young man would retrieve from the warehouse the things he had purchased inside the store and load them in his truck.

Going into town was a luxury for Jack, and as boring as it may sound, the feed store was one of his favorite stops. He always ran into folks he knew there and the banter exchanged with the boys on the dock was a mutually welcomed treat. Conversations about the weather, the almanac predictions for the year, cow breads, dog litters and most things farm related made up the bulk of their conversations. Needless to say, it does not take much to pass for entertainment in a small town.

The conversation had ebbed a bit between Jack and the boys when pulling up to the loading dock beside Jack was an older model half-ton Ford pick-up truck. Evidently the woman from inside the store was now ready to load her purchases. Two very long legs dressed in damn near worn out jeans stepped off the running board of the truck and onto the gravel parking deck. A pony tail was swinging back and forth sticking out the back of an old John Deere ball cap. She wasted no time making her way to the small group standing at the back of Jack's tailgate. She asked with a smile who would be taking her loading ticket?

Jack sat back to enjoy the show. One of those two boys was gonna have to break the trance that had been cast upon them by her unexpected presence and it was going to be interesting to see just how they would handle the situation. It was not every day that a woman ever ventured to the back of the store for loading, certainly not a woman of this highbrow caliber.

The young man Jack knew as Case, jumped to her aid. Ticket in hand, Case began reading off the supplies that he needed to retrieve. Jack found it amusing watching the boys fumbling around loading the nice ladies supplies while she stood at the back of her truck organizing the load to her liking. Jack also noticed something else, the girl did not seem to notice the goofy effect she had on the boys and seemed to be just as down to earth as they were.

This is when Jack's fun came to an end. Instead of being a casual observer, Jack was all of a sudden cast into the fray. As if she were a long lost friend the woman came over and extended a hand to Jack and introduced herself as Kate. Surprised by her boldness, Jack reached out and shook her hand with a firm grip and she reciprocated the gesture.

With a knowing smile Kate said, "And you are Jack Seavers. You own the farm south of my place. It is so nice to finally meet you."

Her warm familiarity of him took Jack by surprise because he was sure he did not know the woman. But Jack quickly followed up with an inquiring tone, "You purchased ole man Ed Whitesell's place did ya? There were rumors that it might be for sale?" The lady nodded in the affirmative never taking her eyes off of Jack. He felt a little unsettled as though she had the upper hand knowing who he was while he still knew nothing about her.

Trying to divert the conversation, Jack pointed at the fencing materials she had purchased and made a query as to her intentions.

"Goats", she said. "I have found myself in possession of three small goats and need to make a small pen for them. Otherwise, they will eat my garden down to nothing."

Jack gave a cursory smile and a knowing nod to go along with her giggly comment. Jack quickly noticed that indeed the girl had purchased all the necessary materials needed to make a fine fence for the stated purpose. The boys, announcing completion of the loading process, handed the loading ticket back to the lady. Kate bid a salutation to all before she jumped onto the truck seat with a free spirited bounce and drove away.

Watching the dust settle behind the woman's truck, the boys slowly made their way to where Jack was still sitting on the tailgate. "Well?" Jack said with a questioning sense of enthusiasm, "What do you boys make of that?"

No one made an attempt to answer Jack's question. It was as though there were no words that could summarize all of the things that could have been said, but couldn't possible explain what they had all just witnessed. Beauty queens building goat pens was a hard thing to explain.

There was still a persistent pause between the men as the boys continued to stare down the road as the truck slowly disappeared from sight. Jack finally spoke again, "She said that her name was Kate and that she purchased the Whitesell farm south of my place."

Still, there was no comment from the other two boys. Jack continued, "She said that she was building a fence for her three goats. Said something about how they were eating her garden." And still there was silence as the boys continued to stare down the road in the direction the lady traveled when she left.

Case finally spoke in a slow contemplative drawl, "She sure was a pretty lady. She was not wearing any kind of make-up."

Case's trusty side kick muttered, "Yeah, and did you see how nice she was to us, not stuck-up or anything."

Jack nodded in agreement.

"Mr. Seavers, do you think she is married?" Case asked.

"Well… she did not have on a wedding band, she came to get fencing without a written materials list that would have typically been given to her by a man if one was around. And she did not flinch to correct me when I inquired if "she" purchased the Whitesell farm instead of admitting to "we" purchased the farm if a man had been part of the equation." Jack explained.

"Gee Mr. Seavers, you are very observant." The young side

kick added. Jack acknowledged the compliment with a smile and bid goodbye to the boys until next weekend.

The drive home was not without Jack being a little preoccupied thinking about this woman. She was pretty he had to admit. But that is not the least of what Jack found attractive about her. He liked her down to earth persona and the way she appeared to appreciate hard work. She walked tall and proud and she appeared to be comfortable in her own skin. She was confident in the way she carried herself and the way she went about her business. She appeared to treat people with respect and she was humbled to do so. Her cologne appeared to be the faint smell of diesel fuel and barn hay. What was not to like? Jack was not the kind of man to chase after women, but that did not mean he could not appreciate a good one when he saw it. And this woman was definitely worth appreciating.

Jack pulled his truck off the road beside his mailbox at the end of his long driveway. Waving in the wind was a slip of paper wedged in the mailbox door. The paper was a receipt from the Feed and Seed Store with fencing materials listed on one side and a note written on the back. The note said, "Jack, please come for supper tonight. I have many questions about the farm and understand you are the best source of information around these parts. Besides, I would really like to know my neighbors better. Supper is at 7. My phone number is on the front of this receipt, please call if you cannot make it. Kate."

Immediately upon reading the note Jack felt... Well, to tell you the truth... Jack did not know how to feel. He could not describe his feelings exactly except to say he was somewhat overwhelmed. Jack had not held the attention of a strange woman in a long time. Too long depending on whom you ask. So Jack was really curious about what might be the lady's true motives for demanding his company. Did she really need his advice about the farm? Was she sincere about meeting ALL of her neighbors?

Then out of nowhere Jack had the fearful notion that maybe, just maybe, she wanted something more personal from Jack? This worried him because Kate looked to be a bit too sophisticated for him on a social level. She was definitely out of Jack's league as far as looks were concerned. And Jack was not about to admit that he, himself, was the actual owner of such an alluring personality and irresistible intellect that could naturally attract women like bees to honey. That thought alone made him laugh out loud with a nervous dose of apprehension.

Realistically, Jack would really like to know his neighbor. He rationalized that it was not like she was asking him for anything out of the ordinary. Neighbors around these parts were known to pitch in and help each other from time to time. Matter of fact, it was a common practice to help your neighbor on occasion. He would also like to enjoy a home cooked meal that he did not cook himself. It was nice to think that he could have a new neighbor to talk with every now and then. And to have a neighbor that wasn't too bad on the eyes was a bonus.

Quickly regaining a sense of sanity, Jack abruptly put the brakes on this runaway train of thinking that was now starting to cause him a little emotional anguish. Jack was a self-made man living a perfectly comfortable, independent life on the farm. He was not about to go looking for anything that would upset the apple cart of his happy, solitary lifestyle.

Jack simply huffed dismissively over the entire subject and figured having a strong back and a knack for putting up goat pens was geared more towards his skill set of attractive features at the moment. This being Jack's final thought, the matter was put behind him for the rest of the day.

It wasn't until Jack had turned down the Whitesell's driveway off the main road did his palms get sweaty. This was confusing to Jack. He had no expectations for their meeting. He did not dress in any particular manner other than his normal farm clothes. Jack made no special preparations or altered himself in any special regard for the supper he was attending. And he certainly was not expecting anything from their meeting except normal discussion about such matters as farmers are bound to talk about. Somehow, his hands were sweaty just the same. Dismissing their betrayal, Jack continued down the driveway until he pulled up to the house.

Ole man Whitesell would have been proud, he thought. The house had a fresh coat of paint on the outside and there was a porch swing at the west end facing the setting sun. Lush ferns were hanging between the front porch post and planter boxes were installed at all the front windows with blooming flowers overflowing their planters. The house looked like something from Southern Living Magazine. Jack was impressed. Kate's white Ford truck was parked out front over to the left side of the yard near the pasture where three small goats were resting comfortably in a newly constructed fenced pen. Jack softly mumbled under his breath, "Well I'll be damned, there is her goat fence."

Jack made his way across the yard to the porch steps when

the screen door to the house flung open and out stepped Kate carrying a tray of ice tea and homemade ginger snap cookies. Jack stopped in his tracks one foot already on the bottom step and his hand resting on the porch rail. Kate's smile was beaming from ear to ear and she embodied beauty that was simple and natural. Kate's long hair was up in the back in a half bun. She was wearing a sleeveless white sun dress that stopped just above her knees. It was decorated with a small pink and rose colored floral print. Her smile, her walk, the graceful way she carried herself seemed genuine and effortless. She was a graceful thing to behold and Jack had never seen anything quite like it.

Trying to gain control over what he thought was an extenuated gaze of admiration, Jack said, "Didn't know I was to dress-up for the occasion?"

Kate smiled at Jack before adding, "Good thing you decided to cover your bones with something or you would have shown up in your birthday suit."

They both laughed out loud as Kate seemed to have broken the ice with her quick wit. Kate followed up her comment by saying, "Jack, if I had to guess, I don't think you own anything much different than what you have on right now. So you are dressed exactly as I expected and you are welcome here anytime."

Jack was not offended by her astute observation. But he was taken by her knowledge of his wardrobe which encouraged Jack to inquire, "Just how do you know so much about my wardrobe? Did you pet my front porch guard dog behind the ears and gain access to snoop around in my closet?"

Kate freely giggled at Jack's comment recognizing his country style of humor. Kate sat the tray of refreshments on a table beside the porch swing and with a warm, inviting smile gestured for Jack to sit. He slowly made his way up the steps and across the porch until he was standing next to Kate who was pouring tea from a pitcher into glasses filled with ice. Kate turned with a full glass and handed it to Jack with instructions for him to have a seat. He did and she sat down beside him with her own glass.

Kate opened the conversation, "Jack, I have been in this town for about three months. Every person here knows you and has only good things to say. Just a casual mention of Jack Seavers and people start talking as if they are privileged to call you a friend. All I did was listen and make mental notes of what was being said. As for your wardrobe, the lady at the General Store said you buy the same clothes regardless of her advice otherwise, and you have not changed your view about men's fashion and style in forever. You don't eat at the dinner often, but when you do it is always the salt and peppered catfish plate with sweet tea. You have two daughters that have married and moved on with their lives. They visit often. You go to the Methodist Church... but not every Sunday. You don't buy many groceries preferring instead to grow and harvest your own food. You are a man of few words and generally speak your mind but are respectful doing so. You are soft spoken and kind and I presume you are a loving and caring soul to anyone you consider family or friend.

"What's your point Kate?" Jack interrupted Kate's rambling while feeling a bit over exposed.

"My point is that I lied to you today and I need to make it right. I don't have many friends here yet and I would very much like to consider you my friend. I realize however, that friends don't tell lies to each other." Kate said.

And for the first time Jack saw Kate without a smile. Kate's eyes were intently searching for Jack's reaction. She had a look of genuine concern and this intrigued Jack.

Jack asked curiously, "Well, given the fact we have actually only met today and have spoken about very little, I cannot imagine what you could have possible said that would have been untrue and so important?"

Kate looked down, thinking about how to rectify the situation. In a straight forward tone, Kate began her explanation. "You see, today you asked me if I purchased this farm. I nodded yes. Well, I did not purchase this farm. My father, Ole man Whitesell as you call him, left it to me. I am his daughter."

Now it was Jack's turn to be embarrassed and have regret over something that had been said. Jack immediately began apologizing for calling Kate's father an "old man." His comment was obviously a derogatory reference about the man's age. However, Kate quickly put her hand on Jack's arm to quieten his concerns of offending her by saying, "My father was old and I know you meant what you said as an expression of kind familiarity not contempt." Jack said nothing but smiled in agreement back at her. Having cleared the air, Kate was smiling again and Jack was relieved that no everlasting harm was done by a few misplaced comments.

Jack questioned, "Kate, I did not know Ole man… I mean, Mr. Whitesell had a daughter? You did not grow up around here so what is the story behind that whole situation if you don't mind me asking?"

Kate laughed out loud and giggled as she spoke, "Well Jack, my mom and dad met when he was in the military stationed in California. She moved to the farm with him and I was born shortly thereafter. But my mom was persistently home sick to the point that she had to move back to California. Dad had to stay here feeling it was his responsibility to look after his aging parents.

Dad loved my mom and me very much, and he was a doting father and faithful husband. But he could only visit us every so often. He was terribly torn between a strong sense of duty in two different directions. I could see he was in a constant state of turmoil as any decision he made would have been wrong either way. He could not be with us full time in California AND take care of his parents and this farm at the same time. He split his time between the two responsibilities the best that he could. He frequently told me stories about this place. Told me how much it meant to him. Said that he was giving it to me as a way to make up for all the time we missed sharing together."

Jack did not realize, until now, how little he knew about Ed Whitesell. Ed stayed to himself mostly and on the few occasions there was interaction between them, Ed seemed like a decent guy always friendly and willing to help a neighbor if needed. The more Jack thought about Kate's story the more what he knew about Ed started to make sense. Like the way he would disappear sometimes and the stand-offish way he acted. Ed was hiding this whole other life. Jack felt a little ashamed that he did not know Ed better. Enough so that he blurted out to Kate, "How did I miss all of this about your dad. How could I have possible been so blind?"

Kate was quick to respond, "It is not your fault. Dad always felt a huge burden of regret for his circumstances of having to live two lives. Maybe in a lot of ways, he thought it easier to avoid judgment by others if he kept to himself. But make no mistake Mr. Jack Seavers, my father admired you very much. He mentioned your name often and I am not sure he realized it, but he was always telling stories about running into you and your family from time to time. He spoke fondly about the close relationship you appeared to have with your daughters and I think he held a certain amount of envy wishing it was he that could have had that same everyday interaction with his own family. I never got the feeling that he was jealous of you. He was maybe just a bit homesick for the relationship he wanted with his family but couldn't have."

Jack looked at Kate with kind eyes and reached out to squeeze her hand resting comfortable in her lap. He gave her a warm smile. Kate smiled back at Jack and continued speaking, "Because my dad spoke so highly of you, I was drawn to find out as much as I could about you from the people in town. I hope that my inquisition was casual enough not to have been obvious or intrusive. Our meeting at the Feed and Seed Store was not by chance. I knew when you would be there as part of your Saturday morning routine in town and made sure to be there as well. I wanted to see you for myself. As for the dinner invitation, that was an uncharacteristic and impulsive thing for me to do and I was so nervous leaving you the note. But now, here you are and I finally get to meet face to face with the man my father admired so much."

Jack was quick to be humbled and said bashfully, "Kate, I am sorry to disappoint you. I am but a simple man, living out here in the country with my dogs, cows and chickens. I feel a bit uncomfortable you making me out to be this bigger than life famous person you have obviously blown out of proportion."

Hearing Jack's confession only made Kate smile that much bigger and she said, "It is adorable that you have not a clue the influence you had on my father and continue to have on other people. The caring way you treat people, the simple, honest way you live your life. Don't you understand, a lot of people look up to you Jack." Kate leaned forward and kissed Jack on the cheek.

If red could be many different colors at one time, Jack turned every shade. He was not accustomed to being fussed over and he most certainly was not used to being kissed unless one of his daughters were doing the honor.

Kate pulled away and stared into his eyes and whispered honestly, "You remind me so much of my Dad. I feel like I know you. I would like to have you in my life for strength, stability and guidance just like my Dad would have given me if he were here.

Jack nervously smiled and said, "guess you do know me pretty well since you went all mission impossible on me in town." Jack's attempt at humor made Kate laugh out loud again. And he added, "I did not realize I was so predictable."

But Kate corrected him sharply, "You are not predictable. You are loving, reliable and stable. You are the trusted father figure I would like to have in my life."

Jack did understand what Kate was trying to say. And Jack felt extremely comfortable with the daughter/ father relationship that was developing between them. He felt more relaxed knowing Kate's true intentions for asking him to supper and was happy to be in her company.

"Kate, what do you hope to gain by being here and do you know yet what your future plans will be?"

Kate thought for a minute before responding, but was quick to flash Jack a knowing, confident look of contentment. Kate spoke warmly, "Jack, I want my journey here to be about discovery. I want to know my father better by living where he lived, knowing the people he knew and enjoying the sights, sounds and smells of this farm just as he did. I want to experience the happiness this place provided for him. I want to discover the magic of this place that, until now, has been a mystery to me. My father was a good, honest, decent man and I want to be like him. This may sound silly, but I can feel my father's presence here and his soul beats in my chest like my own heart beating."

Jack thought about the nobility of her intentions. He could think of no greater way Kate could respect and honor her father except by wanting to know him and live in his shoes. Jack thought about the boots she had been wearing at the Feed Store, and with an appreciative state of understanding, Jack was in agreement that she was indeed walking in her father's footsteps. Kate added, "This may sound silly, but I already feel different. I already feel closer to my dad. I already feel as though I am beginning to know him better. Being here in this town, on this property, in this house is teaching me about my heritage. It's building my character and making me into the person I want to be. I want my Dad to be proud of me. And now, I have you to help support me and show me the way. I am without a doubt the happiest I have ever been in my entire life….. And she was.

The Beauty of Ugly

Evening light cast long shadows on the Seaver's farm. Jack busied himself with last minute chores before going in for the night. As part of his nightly ritual, he secured the milk cow in a barn stall giving her a scoop of sweet feed. She didn't need the extra food; Jack thought giving her the extra sweet snack at bedtime would make the morning milk taste better.

Out of habit, he walked past the electric fence box hung on the barn wall to make sure the energy light was shining brightly. A dim light or no light at all, was a sure sign the fence was not working. He was convinced livestock could tell the difference between a properly charged electric fence and one that sent out invitations to the cattle for exploration beyond its borders. A dead electric fence meant overnight frolicking by any number of escapees. Finding and repairing a fence problem before dark was better than rounding up a rouge bunch of farm animals in the neighbors turnip patch by morning.

Jack made his way around to the side of the barn where he kept the dog food in a little storage room. The door, like the barn itself, was made from rough sawn oak planks that had long since weathered to a faded gray color showing off almost a century's worth of age. Jack reached for and removed the corn cobb stuck in the hasp keeping the door shut. Two thoroughly rusted buckle hinges creaked loudly when he opened the door. He reached into the dog food bag and scooped out a healthy portion of food with an old coffee tin he used as a measuring cup. Tails were vigorously wagging as he put the food into separate bowls. The dogs needed no command to eat but he gave them soft words of encouragement anyway.

By now, the chickens had gone to roost. Jack kicked over the stick that had been holding open the hen house door. He latched the door securely with a bent nail he twisted into place. From there, he took a long walk on a well-worn path that would take him to a water spigot. He gave his cows and horses fresh water every day. Seeing the water trough was now full, he turned off the spigot. From this location, Jack could survey the expansive pastures taking an inventory of the cows and horses scattered about making sure all was well.

Jack entered the rear of his house through a screened door. Actually, he entered into an enclosed porch area that served as a mud room. The back door to the house was a solid door that opened into the kitchen. He left his boots at the door and removed his socks. He kept a chair at the door just for this purpose. Jack liked having bare feet and went bare footed when he could get away with it. He was raised not having shoes as a boy. The eventual introduction to wearing shoes was only a suggestion the way young Jack saw it. His initial resistance to strapping on the uncomfortable clod-hoppers did wain with age and refinement, but that did not mean he was a total convert.

An apron hung on the pantry door. It was made of a heavy cotton material and sported a picture of a barn yard scene with two horses on the front. Like a welder donning protective gear, Jack dutifully pulled the neck strap over his head allowing the side strings to hang loose. A cast iron skillet was about all Jack ever cooked with and the resulting popping and splashing of grease was absorbed by the apron.

A hand full of sizzling bacon was now proving the apron's worth, while Jack rolled out a half dozen homemade biscuits. Cold fresh milk was poured into his favorite tall glass and bits of fine ice crystals gathered at his upper lip when he took a sip. Jack added a few scramble eggs to some of the bacon grease and waited while the cast iron now removed from the stove still cooked the eggs with the residual heat retained by the heavy pan. Breakfast for supper was a common meal at the Seaver's house. It was one of his favorites.

Jack was quick to clean and tidy the kitchen after the satisfying meal was relished and consumed. He often thought about how lucky he was to live such a simple and happy life. He would often bask in the glory of his contentment, and this night was yet another example of the perfect ending to a great day of living life on a farm.

But for some reason, Jack was starting to feel the heavy burden of tension in his shoulders and neck. He did not notice it at first, but caught himself reaching for and rubbing the back of his neck for comfort. This was a sure sign of something important, he quietly admitted to himself.

Jack settled down on the front porch swing and listened to the night sounds of frogs, crickets, and an assortment of screeching and rustling he often heard from the wilderness that surrounded his house. This was his special time to sooth away any mental worries that may have wormed their way into his life. Yet, for some reason… Jack could not say why, he was feeling antsy. He found himself fidgeting with the buttons on his shirt. This was surely a sign and Jack had the strange feeling he was forgetting something.

Jack went inside and sat in his easy chair beside the living room lamp. On the small table beside the chair was a newspaper from the previous week advertising the County Fair coming to town with a half page article describing the event. Jack smiled seeing the advertisement. There weren't many times young Jack ever went to the Fair. Even then, as a boy, he was showing off his pride livestock competing with other country boys for ribbons and in some cases small cash awards for having raised a fine specimen of any certain breed of chicken, horse or cow. The livestock exhibition was his favorite part of the Fair. Jack sat reminiscing with happy memories and smiled when it dawned on him this was the week the Fair was to be in town. He now understood what his pesky subconscious was trying to get him to remember.

The evening was early so Jack decided to make a trip into town for a few hours. It had been a long time since he last went to the Fair. He felt a familiar giddiness from his youth enhance his mood. Jack quickly washed up and changed clothes. He even splashed on a little cologne feeling especially worthy of a night away from the farm… and not wanting to smell like one too.

Jack could feel the electricity of excitement as soon as he pulled into the parking lot. The jovial music, the flashing lights, the food smells, the noise of the crowd all contributed to jolting Jack's senses into awareness. It is sometimes hard to distinguish if the mood of excitement is energy you can feel from other people or the result of your own expectations, or maybe both. Either way, Jack was smiling.

Jack paid admission and began a slow, casual saunter around the well-organized rows of games, shows, contests, food, and rides. While he wanted to eventually work his way to the livestock barn, he was not in a hurry to get there. Jack was happy to enjoy the energetic atmosphere of the Fair at his own pace.

He soon found himself standing and watching the plate breaking game. A local High School baseball pitcher had stepped up to the counter to throw his luck. Everyone was eagerly anticipating the pitcher bankrupting the carny of his largest stuffed animals. The larger bears were the prize for knocking over and breaking five plates out of five attempts. Most participants opted for the three-ball-throw as that was a cheaper option of play and had a higher possibility for success. However, the prize for winning was not very impressive.

Jack watched as the High school pitcher played four games of the five-out-of-five variety trying to win the biggest prize. But to the dismay of the crowd and especially to the pitcher himself, he failed with much disappointment. Jack overheard a tall lanky young man in the crowd turn to his girlfriend and say, "Heck, if he can't do it I don't stand a chance."

Jack reached out and put a hand on the young man's shoulder. He asked confidently, "Son, would you like to win a big bear for your lady friend?" The boy looked at Jack with a bit of uncertainty in his skills to risk losing his pride to failure. Jack gave him a calm look of confidence and smiled, "Son, if you are willing to try, I can give you some pointers that will help you win at this game." The young man looked at his girlfriend and saw hope and expectation in her eyes. He knew he could not say no. His pride was on trial whether he wanted it to be or not. The boy looked back at Jack with a blank expression. Jack simply said, "come with me, I will pay for you to play. I have confidence in you."

Jack and the boy walked up to the bench. The carny was shouting encouragement to the demoralized crowd as the High School pitcher walked away empty handed. Jack said to the carny, "This young man would like to try." The carny looked at Jack as he pushed forward his hand with the correct amount of money for admission clearly on display. The carny took the money and presented five baseballs to the young man with a smirk.

Seeing doubt in the boy's eyes, Jack leaned over and whispered into his ear. "Son, this game is rigged, here is how you beat it. Don't stand in the middle to play. There are bright lights on the targets and on you that will throw off your depth perception. Stand to either side to throw. Next, throw at the plates on the ends of the rows. Most of the end plates are real plates and will break easily. The plates in the middle won't break if you took a sledge hammer to them. He can't even reach the middle plates if he had to replace them so you know they have to be fake. Next, the game plates that cannot be broken have a small red label on them. Aim for the end plates without the red label. Those are the disposable, breakable plates. Lastly, this is our secret. It wouldn't be fair to ruin the carny's night by giving away his advantages to everyone."

Jack turned without saying another word and casually continued his walk. He didn't get far when he heard the roar of a jubilant crowd. He did not even look back; Jack smiled knowing the young man was a plate breaking winner.

Laughter, giggles and squeals were coming from all directions. This made Jack happy. He understood the County Fair was a business entity selling entertainment. Even if most of it were disguised as fair play and honest chance, entertainment still cost money so even the losers were winners.

Jack wondered into the section organized for rides. He was fortunate enough to ride horses on his farm anytime he desired. Jack liked riding. But spinning in circles and being jerked around up and down was not exactly what he considered as fun. The kids however, seemed to love it. Jack stood watching their smiling faces and hearing their squeals and screams of happiness as they were jostled back and forth in their seats.

A family was also slowly making their way down the lane between the rides. Jack saw the man with a short roll of tickets in his hand with a wife and four children in tow. A little boy pulled on the man's shirt tail pointing to a certain ride. The man looked at his tickets and regretfully shook his head no to the boy. This gave Jack an idea. He quickly found a ticket booth and purchased two handfuls of tickets. He then doubled back and found the family still walking slow holding hands together looking at all the ride possibilities. Jack introduced himself to the man and explained that his daughter was feeling ill and needed to go home. Since the tickets were non-refundable, Jack asked the man if he would use the tickets instead.

Jack was again on his way. It wasn't long when he rounded a corner and took notice of a young mother standing near the spinning swings. She was holding what looked like a two year old and was waiting for her son to exit the ride when it was over. He noticed the youngster in her arms was smiling at him. Jack paused for a second to smile back. The child began reaching for him and the mother turned to see what was going on behind her back. Jack stood motionless, smiling with his usual bashful self. The mother saw Jack and realized his appearance was warm and kind. She said to Jack, "Beth does not usually take to strangers. I am surprised she wants to go to you." Feeling comfortable with the mother's friendly attitude, Jack covered his hands over his eyes and played peek-a-boo with the child. To a chorus of infectious giggles, Jack told the lady he had raised two daughters of his own and lamented how he missed interacting with them at that age.

The little girl reached out vigorously for Jack to hold her. The woman was obviously surprised and a bit apprehensive with the child's behavior. Looking at Jack she saw warmth and kindness in his eyes. She even surprised herself when she heard words escape from her own mouth asking Jack if he wanted to hold the girl for a moment while she retrieved her son now exiting the ride.

Jack smiled and dutifully declined her kind gesture. That's when the child pushed hard with her legs and leapt from her mother's arms towards Jack reaching for him. Jack lunged forward to catch the child now tumbling out of her mother's arms toward the ground. With one large hand Jack collected the baby now safely cradled in his gentle grasp.

A person would expect the exasperated moment to have startled the child. But no, it was as if the leap of faith were all part of the happy game she was playing with him. The mother, on the other hand, was bewildered at the insistence of the child to escape from her arms. Jack immediately gestured forward the child in his hands giving her back to the mother who was thankful for Jack's quick reflexes. But the mother simply said with an obvious hint of humor, "Oh no mister, you have her now you get to keep her." The woman softly smiled and touched Jack's arm as a gesture of acceptance.

While it had been a long time since Jack held a child, he did so with competent experience. The squirming bundle of giggles proved to be a surprising challenge but Jack was not deterred. He quickly reached into his pocket and retrieved his keys. He made a jingling noise in front of the baby's face and handed them to the girl to play with. This new toy was enough to occupy the baby while Jack introduced himself to the mother. Small talk ensued for a minute or two when Jack thanked her for her kindness and handed the girl back. The baby didn't cry but was clearly not happy about leaving Jack's company. Jack always had a soft spot in his heart for dogs and children and he always seemed to be popular with both.

Walking away, Jack thought back to the woman's son. He was quiet but seemed to be enjoying the Fair with a look of reserved bashfulness. Jack noticed his pants were high watered showing his ankles and his hand-me-down looking shirt was too big for his thin frame and was bunched up around his belt tucked into his pants. Jack smiled to himself contently thinking about how the woman could likely use the two hundred dollars he slipped into the baby's coat pocket. Jack reasoned the young woman might as well have the money because he had no use for it at the moment.

Bellowing cows, pig grunts, and the pungent smell of hay and livestock reminded Jack why he had come to the Fair. Turning another corner Jack found himself in a well-lit graveled lot. The exhibition barn and many animal pens surrounding it were close at hand. Small groups of boys and men dotted the farmyard. Jack easily recognized most of them and gave a friendly wave of his hand or a tip of his hat as he past them.

Jack looked down the row of holding pens where the cows were kept on display. Standing at the side of each pen was a young boy beaming with pride. The sight made Jack smile remembering his youthful County Fair experiences; he could almost feel the butterflies he knew were in the stomachs of each one of those young men.

Inviting other people to scrutinize what you have worked so hard to achieve is a humbling experience. It's not easy being judged. Jack understood the elation of winning, but he also thought it was a more important life lesson to lose. There would be much heartache and disappointment for those young men who would not have their hard work validated with a first, second or third place ribbon. Jack knew too well the painful emotional process for those boys who lost. The inner strength used by each young man to overcome their feelings of rejection and failure would be the same foundation they would use later in life to build strong character and a successful attitude.

Jack shook the hand of each young man when he stopped to admire their prized calf. He gave each boy his undivided attention and took a genuine interest in their conversation. Jack naturally gave words of encouragement to each boy and a pat on the back was his signatory salutation.

It was however, the last pen at the end of the row that interested Jack the most. He saw none of the other spectators stopping to visit this contestant. The boy at this pen was a bit younger than the rest of the other boys in the contest. And while a bit of anxiety should be expected for a young boy showing off his hard work and effort to public scrutiny, the boy just looked exhausted with rejection.

Jack took notice of the calf as the boy walked up to greet him. "Son, my name is Jack Seavers and I want to see your young bull." An apprehensive smile did manage to curl at the ends of the boy's lips when he shook Jack's hand.

Jack turned to focus attention on the prized animal, but there wasn't much to look at. The bull calf was half the size he should have been for his age. You couldn't count every rib, but the calf was not as fat as he could have been. Jack also noticed the animal moved around with a limp.

"Mister, this is my bull, Jake. I know he looks bad. He has had a hard life so far. When he was born, he developed BVD (bovine viral diarrhea). It was a severe case. The vet wanted to put him down, but I begged for a chance to make him better. I gave him bottles even when he did not want to eat. I gave him his medicine when he was supposed to have it. I made him get up and walk around every day to give him strength. Mister, Jake didn't know he wanted to live, I had to teach him."

The boy enthusiastically climbed over the gate and went to the calf's side. He stood close to the calf leaning against the young bull with his hip and put his arm around his neck. The boy looked pensive for a second before explaining further. "Ole Jake was doing good too, before he was chased down by two of the neighbor's dogs that thought Jake was a play toy. They chased him into some barbed wire fencing. He got tangled in the fence pretty bad. The dogs were biting at him. The boy paused and looked down with a strained expression as if it was hurting him to remember.

Jack noticed a woman casually walking up to the side of the pen as the boy was talking. She listened to her son tell his story. The boy acknowledged her presence with a swift look in her direction, but quickly looked back at Jack and continued speaking. "Mister, I was so scared for Jake and so mad at those dogs. I picked up a tobacco stick from the barn and walloped them over the head trying to get them to stop barking and biting at

Jake. After a few whacks and a broken stick, they finally ran off. That's how Jake got that scar on his shoulder." Jack looked and indeed saw the remnants of an ugly, jagged scare about six inches long where the bull's neck met his right front shoulder.

"Mister, would you believe he got a screw stuck in his foot last week. I saw him limping and got my dad to help me hold him down. We pulled out the screw and sprayed his foot with antiseptic. I melted some pine tar in a tuna can to cover the hole in his hoof trying to keep out infection." Jack hopped the fence too and pulled up the bull's foot to inspect the wound. "Son, that's a perfect patch. You do good work."

The boy gave Jack a bashful smile before continuing to speak. "Daddy said we have to get rid of Jake. Said Jake was a runt, wasn't good for nothing. But sir, it's not his fault he's ugly. He can't help it he got sick and his growth was stunted or that he walks with a limp. Jake doesn't think nothin's wrong with his foot anymore. He really is a happy calf as long as I keep the dogs off him."

Jack noticed how much the boy needed to tell his story. How much the boy needed for someone else to see his beautiful calf the way he saw him. Jack noticed the apologetic tone of the boy's voice when he spoke as if the boy himself were to blame for all the struggles that had befallen upon the bull's young life. Jack noticed how the boy was always quick to disregard his own heroic contributions to better the quality of life for Jake against what was clearly an unfortunate string of bad luck for the struggling animal. The young man took his responsibilities serious and was humble far beyond his years.

Jack looked up and saw a tear stream down the boy's face. His mother quietly cupped her hand over her mouth to choke back her own emotions. The boy said to Jack with a sincere pleading for understanding in his voice, "Mister, Jake deserves to be at the Fair too, he doesn't know he is ugly."

Jack is happy with his life. He lives on a working farm where he gets much joy out of doing everyday simple things. His favorite time of day is when he puts the farm animals to bed each night. He checks the light on the electric fence box like always. He feeds the dogs from an old coffee can. He makes sure to fill the water trough for the livestock in the pasture. And he closes and secures the chicken coop door with a rusty, bent nail. Only now, Jack makes two scoops of sweet feed, one for his dairy cow and one for Jake.

Perfect in my Eyes

Jack did not need an alarm to wake him. It was the first day of a new deer season and he was too excited to sleep. He lay in bed with his eyes relaxed and closed, but his mind was racing with anticipation. The room was cool as Jack heated his home with a fireplace and the fire had long burned itself out. Jack could feel the chill in the air on the tips of his nose and ears. It was mid-October and fall weather had arrived cool and dry making for perfect deer hunting weather. The hot, humid dog days of late summer were finally over and Jack was glad about that.

Even though it was time for Jack to get up, he lay in bed enjoying the cozy warmth just a little bit more before having to put his feet onto the hard, cold floor just yet. Something about the weight of a heavy quilt and the warmth trapped against you that feels so inviting to stay put a minute or two longer. It is as if the heft of the blankets are trying to hold you down warning you to stay in bed or suffer the unkind consequences of the cold waiting to assault you.

Jack pushed the mound of bedding off to one side allowing the cool air of the room to rush into his warm sanctuary. He twisted his legs over the side of the bed and his feet hit the floor with a mild thump. He half expected the cold floorboards to soak through the soles of his feet and run a chill up his spine. Jack went bare-footed most of his life therefor his feet were desensitized to the harsh environment of the cold floor. He hardly noticed. What did catch Jack by surprise was the cold tap water from the bathroom sink when he washed his face and brushed his teeth. He inspected the faucet half expecting to see icicles hanging from the tap.

Jack shuffled toward the kitchen humming a happy tune. First things first, he thought, as he started heating the coffee pot on the stove. His clothes had been carefully laid out the night before on the kitchen table. Each article of clothing was in the exact order they needed to be when he dressed. Jack was meticulous about layering his clothing expecting to stay warm and dry during the cold morning hunt. Being comfortable also meant being able to take clothes off later in the morning once things warmed up a bit. Jack had been through this dressing ritual many times over the years and now he seemed to do it without much thought.

After dressing, Jack wandered over to the coffee pot that was announcing its readiness. The cup was warm in Jack's hands when he brought the steaming mug to his nose and took a deep breath of the aromatic goodness that was to come. He smiled before taking the first sip as if the anticipation was as good as the coffee itself. "Ahhh"- was all Jack could think upon taking that first tasty bit of roasted flavor on his lips and tongue. "Just does not get much better than this," Jack said as he smiled to himself.

Jack reached into the fridge and pulled out a plate of precooked sausage patties to go with a few fluffy homemade biscuits. The biscuits were leftovers he had intentionally saved from his supper the night before. A couple sausage biscuits were just the thing to go with his coffee to make breakfast quick and satisfying. And it was.

With a second hot cup of joe in hand, Jack shuffled his way into the living room. Awaiting his inspection was a small pile of dwindling ash in the fireplace from the fire Jack enjoyed just a few hours earlier. Jack could not say for sure who coined the phrase "all good things must end," but he was confident they must have been talking about the ill fate of a roaring fire. All fires start out warm, bright, colorful and full of promise and they all end up a dingy, dirty pile of cold soot and ash.

Jack smiled thinking about the circle of life. How he would later dump the ash in the garden and it would serve to fertilize next year's new crop of fruits and vegetables. Finding value and purpose in all things no matter how small or insignificant was the way Jack lived his life. Some folks may have called him simple, but Jack didn't mind being labeled as simple. He appreciated knowing how to live off the land and he took a sense of pride understanding nature's essence at its most basic levels.

Poking around in the ashes, Jack managed to regain a small puff of smoke and a marginal flame with the last bit of hot embers that still remained. Jack then headed toward the chair at his desk. On the way, he opened the cedar wood door to the gun cabinet and retrieved his longtime friend. It was a Winchester 30-30 rifle he had purchased a long time ago when he was a younger man. Back then, he was just starting out in life. He did not have a lot of money and could not afford much else. He remembered how he purchased the gun for next to nothing from a local dairy farmer who was briefly down on his luck.

He also remembered how the damn thing would not shoot worth a toot until he removed the cheap scope that had been mounted on the little gun. He never put another scope back on it, choosing instead to use the iron sights. And that is when the magic happened. As it turned out, the little gun was deadly accurate. So Jack has been shooting it with iron sights ever since.

Jack sat in the chair next to his desk. He held the gun in his hands and admired the rich oil stained mahogany colored wood stock. He smiled thinking what a thing of beauty it was: scratches, dents, and dings were soothing reminders of their past adventures together. Sure, Jack had a collection of other guns he could have selected for this hunt, but he was drawn to the little gun out of nostalgic reverence and thought it would be the perfect companion to start the new season.

With familiar repetition, Jack pulled open the top drawer of the desk and retrieved an oil rag he kept there. He held the rifle gingerly and polished it with a sense of satisfaction. The gun did not need to be oiled as much as Jack needed to oil it. None-the-less, both Jack and the gun were soon shining with a handsome glow. There was never a time when the pair were together that they did not shine brightly with natural luster.

Jack stood from his chair and finished dressing for the hunt that was now urgently calling for his attention. He grabbed his old hunting coat from the closet and realized it still had the trappings of September's dove season within it. There were a few 16 gauge shells in the pockets and downy dove feathers were puffing into the air from the game pouch in the back. Jack admired the coat with dignity and shook his head as he remembered his promise to wash the jacket as soon as dove hunting season had ended. A repeating promise he had made to himself over the course of many years of hunting seasons but could never bring himself to actually do it. Smudges of dried blood, dirt, mud stains, and an assortment of small sticks, twigs, and dried leaves that had collected in the bottom of the pockets were all reminders of the times Jack spent afield doing what he loved. Putting on the jacket was like a warm, friendly embrace to Jack. The jacket was comforting to his soul as he was now surrounded by the evidence of how he chose to live his life.

Stepping out the door onto the porch and out into the yard, Jack stopped and gave a knowing smile toward the sky. Night was struggling to hold on a minute or two longer while daylight was beginning to take over. Daybreak would soon happen without making a sound and only those folks quick enough to know what to look for would see it happen. Jack had seen the miracle of daybreak many times and each one was more beautiful than the last. The sky above would first streak with a hint of gold, yellow and orange color while the ground below would still be covered in dark grey and a shimmering hint of ghostly silver. Night would eventually yield to the dawn of a new day and a million natural colors would sprinkle upon the earth once again. It was a sight Jack never got tired of seeing.

The still morning air was crisp and clean. Frost had settled overnight upon the landscape and Jack marveled at the white snow-like appearance. Tall grass covered with ice crystals made a course, rustling sound as he walked through it. Nature was not yet awake and the early morning was still eerily quiet. Jack's footsteps onto the frosty grass crunched with each step. The resulting noise so loud Jack considered the crunching a disturbance to the tranquil stillness of the morning. Jack subconsciously began to walk more slowly trying to quieten the crunching sound of the frost to preserve nature's natural order.

Jack made his way around a large Hay field walking close to the edge trying to reduce his silhouette to wild roaming eyes. He walked with the wind in his face knowing this would keep his scent from reaching the flaring nostrils of the deer he was hunting. Jack crossed a bubbling creek at one of only two crossings on his property that was shallow enough for him not to fill the tops of his boots with ice water. Daylight was a little brighter now and Jack started the portion of his journey that would take him through the woods. He had to navigate around an outcropping of dense cedar saplings and work his way across a hardwood hill of oaks and hickory trees before he reached the place where he wanted to stop and sit to wait out the rest of daybreak before continuing his stalk.

Jack had been hearing lately from the neighboring farmers how they have been seeing an unusually large buck in the area. The animal had been sighted in their fields during the course of harvesting soybeans and corn for the season. Jack knew the animal well because he too had seen him many times. Jack however, knew something about the buck no one else knew- he only lived on Jack's farm during hunting season. Jack had been studying the buck since he was a yearling. Their paths crossed many times over the years. Now the buck was large enough to be considered the regal king of Clay County.

However, as the buck got older he also grew wiser. He developed a knack for survival. He seemed to have learned all the tricks required for staying alive and was keenly smarter than most bucks Jack had ever hunted. This buck would go nocturnal at the first sound of gunfire and he bedded in the thick swamp on the north end of his farm. If this buck was to be killed by a hunter, it would have to be Jack to do it. There were few people having permission to hunt his farm and no one would go to the trouble to hunt the swamp. The swamp was too darn hard to access for all but the most dedicated of hunters and Jack's determination and dedication had no equal.

Jack stopped and sat for a moment when he came to the opening of another long Hay field he needed to cross before accessing the swamp. He sat very still on the wood's edge camouflaged against a large oak tree. A new day began to come alive. Song birds were the first to break the night silence. A random chirp here and there soon turned into a full chorus of cheerful song. Crows could be heard in the distance cowling their morning calls. Squirrels hurriedly jumped from limb to limb heading toward the nearest oak trees still offering a bountiful supply of acorns. Within what seemed like a few short minutes, total quiet bloomed into chaos. Life exploded from the trees, the bushes, the leaves, and from the water of nearby ponds and creeks. A carefully orchestrated dance of a thousand natural puzzles fit themselves together to form the whole picture of what we think about when we view nature.

Too often humans don't see the connected order of life co-existing as a million separate parts coming together as one. Like the sunrise, the magic of seeing the natural world in perfect harmony first requires an understanding of what to look for and the willingness to accept nature the way it really is. Seeing the beauty in nature requires that you look for the things that may not always be so obvious.   Only then can a person understand the natural order of nature and YOUR place as part of that mosaic puzzle. Jack understood.

It was time for Jack to move to the outer edge of the swamp on the east side of the hayfield. There, he knew of a game trail that ventured under the briars and through an overgrown tangle of vines and sumac that normally restricted access within the oasis Jack was seeking. Once through the tangled barrier, there would be a two acre opening of dry land surrounded on all other sides by shallow water. To Jack's knowledge, he was the only person knowing about this spot. If he was correct in his assessment, the buck would show himself within the next thirty minutes or so from the west with the intentions of bedding down for the day. Jack was nervously excited as the prospect of their meeting was now close at hand.

Jack entered the buck's lair quietly and positioned himself against a massive poplar tree. He broke off a few cedar limbs and stuck them into the ground in front of where he was to sit. Jack foraged around for dried leaves and other vegetation to further blend the cedar branches into a natural looking blind to conceal his location from the buck's view. This was no ordinary buck and Jack knew that if he were to outsmart him, he could leave no detail to chance.

Satisfied with the makeshift blind, Jack sat leaning with his back against the trunk of the tree. The open grassy savannah of dry land in front of him was mostly covered with sage grass and some dog fennel. A cluster of dried poke berry stalks were holding claim to their place in the plot at the far left corner. A sizable patch of wild lespedeza occupied the middle section and a nasty tangle of blackberry briers were directly opposite Jack on the far side. Tupelo trees separated the dry land from the swamp and two small cedar saplings were managing to spring forth their claim of belonging to the area and were located immediately to Jack's left. But they did not obstruct his view.

Jack sat quiet… still… watching…. listening…. breathing. All of his senses were focused on being transformed and molded into the fabric of his surroundings. Jack's initial disturbance to the wilderness when he entered the area was starting fade. Nature was returning to its normal tempo of liveliness. A warbler landed on the end of Jack's gun barrel while the gun rested in his lap. Jack smiled. His spirit was now in sync with the wilderness around him and he felt at peace.

The first sign that alerted Jack something could be headed his way, was the barking of squirrels. Their barking was faint and

he could barely hear it over the other wildlife sounds filling the air. But what made the barking squirrels stand out as a sign of significance was their enthusiasm for the effort. Jack understood barking squirrel behavior and was on alert that something was causing a disturbance to their peaceful morning tranquility. Jack listened closely trying to understand their intent.

After a few minutes, the next clue that something could be coming, was the sound of wood ducks lifting off of the swamp water with a cascade of splashing wings and high-pitched whistling that was as urgent as screaming. Jack had heard these duck sounds many times before and knew them to be the sounds of an urgent departure.

But it was not until a pair of cardinals took hurried flight from a holly bush across the grassy meadow and the woods became eerily silent, that Jack began to get nervous with anticipation. His mouth became dry and his hands were shaking with excitement. Jack instinctively clutched the rifle close to his chest with both hands and looked past the barrel with an attentive stare. The silence of the surrounding swamp was deafening and the only sound Jack could hear was the pounding of his own heartbeat in his ears.

There was an unsettled, nervous feeling in the air. Jack felt like he was being watched. He dare not move a muscle. He was afraid to even blink. He was hoping the makeshift blind he had constructed earlier was adequate enough to break up his human form and fool the buck's visual inspection for danger.

Time had now stopped and held no meaning. There is no value of time when you are living in the moment. The moment was unfolding right now and Jack understood the strategic significance of allowing the moment to happen at its own pace. Moments are going to be what they are going to be and this moment was still being determined.

Jack carefully scanned the outermost wood's edge opposite his location. His eyes were searching trying to detect the slightest movement. Deer are sometimes like ghosts and could appear out of thin air. Jack understood this principle and knew he needed to get a better jump on seeing this buck before he fully entered the overgrown grassy savannah to bed.

Keeping his head still, Jack only moved his eyes while scanning for signs of the buck. "He is near, I can feel it," Jack said quietly to himself. Using advice he often gave to young hunters, Jack began searching through the tangles of underbrush and bushes for parts and pieces of the deer instead of a complete image of what he expected to find. The buck did not get to be an old monarch by being stupid. Even though this swamp was his safe sanctuary, he was not about to burst into the open without stopping to scan the area for danger first. Jack was confident he must be standing at the bordering edge looking, smelling and listening for the slightest detail that seemed out of place before entering the sanctuary.

The shot was loud and unexpected. Bolting out of the woods near the blackberry thicket was his buck. The buck stumbled to the ground then tried to get up. He stumbled down again and finally came to rest about 30 yards away from where Jack was hiding. Jack could easily see one side of the buck's grand antlers sticking up above the tall grass.

Jack sat still, quietly trying to deal with his excited state of confusion about what just happened. Bursting through the same opening the buck came from was another hunter running after the buck. The hunter stopped short when seeing the animal and held their gun tentatively ready to shoot again should the animal not be dead.

Jack held his breath and also held tight in his hidden position to see what would happen next. The hunter, having determined the buck had indeed expired, fell upon its body with an exhausted collapse. Without notice to the buck's large set of antlers, the hunter wrapped their arms around the buck's neck and hugged the animal with much affection. Jack heard muffled sobbing, crying sounds coming from the other hunter as they held onto the deer tightly. It was clearly an emotional outpouring. Jack could see the shoulders of the other hunter heaving back and forth with each sobbing catch of breath.

Jack was also trying to gain control of his own emotions. In just an instant, Jack's emotions went from extreme surprise, to confusion, to anger, then to confusion again. And now Jack's feelings of curious sympathy were being tugged by his heart for reasons he did not fully understand. The view unfolding before him was so emotional it was uncomfortable for Jack to watch.

Jack quietly stood and carefully closed the distance between them. He stopped to evaluate the situation further. Still unnoticed, Jack stood with a better view. The other hunter appeared to be small, maybe not more than five feet tall. Even with the bulk of winter clothing covering most of their frame, Jack could see the skinny arms and hands that stuck out from underneath the oversized cuffs of their jacket.

Jack looked closer and noticed this was not just any winter coat the other hunter was wearing. This was a man's dark brown, almost black, wool tweed suit jacket that was initially designed to have been worn to church, or fancy dinner, or someplace where a man might be required to dress nicely. And while fine fashion may have been the intent of the suit maker, the jacket was not being used for that purpose. It was obviously being worn to keep the hunter warm and dry on this cold day.

Jack also noticed that the jacket was ripped at the pocket. Briars had picked at the sleeves leaving a fuzzy texture on the forearms. Every button except one appeared to be missing and the jacket hung open and looked oversized on the small hunter. Some of the interior lining appeared to have come loose and was hanging out a little in the rear. Jack could not begin to understand the many different purposes the jacket may have served over the course of its useful life, but he could easily see how it was being used lately and appreciated the utility.

Jack moved closer and was now about 20 feet away and could clearly hear the sobbing had quieted, and the hunter was in a calmer disposition. The hunter's arms released their hugging grip from the deer's neck and the hunter rose to a kneeling position at the deer's side. With trembling hands, the hunter combed the deer's hide with caring strokes of affection. Jack stopped once more and stood quietly to observe the situation. It impressed Jack to witness a hunter that appreciated the animal more than the antlers.

Using a calm tone, Jack called out to the hunter saying, "Sure is a nice buck."

Jack's words caught the other hunter by surprise. Bouncing to their feet and swiftly turning, the other hunter now faced Jack for the first time. Standing in place, the hunter lowered their head and apologetically stared at the ground while respectfully removing their cap and holding it with both hands.

Jack now recognized the girl when all that blonde hair tumbled from under the hat onto her shoulders. Jack called to her, "Kaylee, is that you?"

"Yes Mr. Seavers, it is me, Kaylee," the girl said with a cracking in her voice and a shortness of breath. Before Jack could respond, the girl burst into tears as she stood still, ready to accept her punishment for having trespassed onto Jack's land. Jack walked up to the girl and took her into his arms. He held her tight and with calm reassuring words, he told her it was okay. Everything was gonna be okay.

Jack could feel the girl in his arms to be nothing but bones and he saw for the first time how her suit jacket literally did swallow her whole. Kaylee had dark circles around her eyes, sunken cheeks and thin lips. Jack could feel his own emotions welling up into his throat and he had to swallow hard to keep them tamped down. Kaylee was a pretty girl but clearly looked as if she had been living on hard times.

Kaylee calmed herself in Jack's embrace. After a moment, she casually pulled away wiping at the wetness on her cheeks and her runny, cold nose with the sleeves of her jacket before looking up at Jack. She began to apologize for having trespassed onto his land and for poaching a deer. But jack quickly interrupted her and sternly asked, "Kaylee, where is your brother, Sonny?" Of all the things Jack could have said or asked of her, nothing would have struck such a tender nerve as to have asked about her brother.

Kaylee fell back into his arms exhausted with emotion. Again, Jack held on to her tightly trying to calm her heaving breaths and shaking shoulders. Jack can't say exactly how he knew her brother was no longer living with the family, but he knew Kaylee would not be out hunting for food if he had still been living at home.

Kaylee lived on the North side of Jack's property on a small two acre plot. She lived with her mother, her older brother Sonny, and her two much younger siblings. Their father passed away about two years ago. At seventeen years old, Sonny instantly became the man of the house. Kaylee fourteen, became an instant babysitter, housemaid and cook while their mother worked as a custodian at the local motel to make ends meat. Sonny worked at the lumber yard and made good money. But like his mother, had to work long and hard hours.

With her arms folded tightly to her chest while wrapped in Jack's embrace, Kaylee told him that Sonny had joined the Marines about six months ago and was soon called up for deployment. She had not heard from him since. She explained how she was scared for her brother. She was not even sure where he was stationed at the moment.

Jack now understood completely the circumstances leading up to this moment. Kaylee had been feeling the tremendous burden and responsibility on her shoulders for her family's well-being and its weight was heavy on her mind. That very much explains the outpouring of gratefulness Kaylee had for having taken the buck. That deer meant the world to Kaylee and her family as it represented much needed food for their winter pantry.

Jack closed his eyes tightly trying to hold back his emotions. He felt guilty and angry with himself that he had not noticed this family's desperate need sooner. Jack's heart melted with anguish causing him to squeeze Kaylee a little tighter absentmindedly lifting her feet off the ground. It hurt Jack to think about Kaylee's family and the hardships they must now be facing. Naturally, Jack's perspective was now clear and determined. Having broad responsible shoulders and with bold intent, it was now Jack's turn to carry some of the weight.

"Kaylee," Jack said with much glee and admiration in his voice. "I am so proud of you. You have taken a fine buck. Probably one of the best bucks I have ever seen."

Kaylee pulled her cheek off of Jack's chest to look up at him and smiled.

Jack continued, "I would love to hear your story about how you out-smarted this wise, old deer."

Kaylee did not hear anger or disappointment in Jack's voice and was perceptive enough to understand that Jack was truly impressed with her hunting skills and that he was not angry about her trespass. With much relief and excitement, Kaylee told Jack about how she had watched the deer cross onto Jack's property every morning at about the same time. She felt confident that she could bag the buck if she could keep her scent out of his nose. She maneuvered along the outer edge of the thick swamp and found a position she thought would put her in shooting range of the deer passing as it went to bed. "And that, Mr. Seavers, is really all I had to do," she said with a beautiful, bashful smile trying to conceal her accomplishment.

Jack was impressed. Even more impressed when he looked down and saw the little gun she had used to take the buck. The gun was a very old single barreled 20ga. shotgun. The gun looked as though it had about two rolls of black electrical tape holding the stock and forearm together and it had a light dusting of surface rust giving the finish a light brown appearance. Just goes to show that it does not take fancy guns and clothes or expensive equipment to kill a monster buck. One just needs to use good common sense and some woodsman ship to get the job done.

At the end of a very long day, Jack found himself occupied with the nightly ritual of poking at glowing embers and hot, dancing flames in the fireplace. He was tired but happy. He thought about how unique this first day of deer season was compared to all the others he had ever experienced. He gazed into the fire trying to burn today's events into his memory. He smiled to himself with a sense of satisfaction.

He remembered how he was able to help Kaylee's family with a load of firewood. Jack remembered how the family was so thankful for a bountiful harvest of venison. He remembered fixing a few things around their house that needed repair. And Jack's offering to make a few calls to follow up on Sonny meant the world to Kaylee's family.

Jack continued to stare into the fire and poked at the wood as he recalled the joy on their faces when he left for the day. He could feel the warmth of their hearts glowing inside of him. It is not a difficult thing to care, and for Jack, his humble reward was the joy of knowing he was able to improve the circumstances for his neighbors if just for a little while.

Jack moved over to the desk and sat down. He absentmindedly reached into the top drawer and pulled out the familiar oiled

rag he would use to clean his new gun before storing it for the night. As he wiped down the barrel, he thought about how he would one day take off all the black electrical tape and give the old 20ga. a much needed refurbishing. Jack secretly knew however, that he would never change a thing about that little gun. In his eyes, it was perfect.

Jack stood from his desk and walked past the fireplace to the closet. He took out a hanger and put away his new hunting jacket. It had a torn pocket, all the buttons were missing except one, and the lining was hanging down in the back. He will forever remember with great fondness, how the suit jacket looked on Kaylee as it swallowed her completely. He was proud to own it as it made him feel warm and happy inside. Kaylee put up a fight protecting her pride when he tried to give her his gun and hunting jacket. She finally agreed to an even trade when she saw how important it was to Jack that she have a proper hunting gun and coat. Jack will always remember her smiling face, her stubborn pride, and her genuine gratitude for the trade.

People say that Jack is but a simple man living a simple life. Many envy his lifestyle. However, Jack knows better. It took the courage, strength and determination of a sixteen year old girl to remind Jack that being simple out of necessity is not the same as being simple by choice. That little girl taught Jack that even in the face of overwhelming misfortune, you can still have pride, dignity, love and respect at the core of who you are and how you live your life. And if being simple also means that you have more room for a huge caring heart… Well, Jack is the proud owner of a new gun and coat.

The Way It Used to Be

Jack sat comfortably in a deer stand high above the forest floor appreciating another glorious day. Autumn's bright colors cascaded across the landscape and a soft cool breeze made the leaves twinkle as if they were dancing in place. Jack looked across the valley and was amazed at how the entire horizon appeared to be on fire as the red, orange, crimson and yellow leaves waved back and forth in the wind creating a busy blaze of movement.

Autumn was Jack's favorite time of year. He was not sure if it was the cool crisp air, the splendor of fall's brilliant colors, the warm smell of smoke from burning firewood, or the bountiful tasty harvest of sweet potatoes, pecans, apples and pumpkins that Jack liked the most. All these things were part of the exclusive nature of what made autumn special.

Jack sat almost overwhelmed with glee as he soaked in the experience. This was one of the rare moments he wished he could preserve in a bottle to share with others as if the experience was too big, the moment too grand to be wasted only for him. For no apparent reason, Jack noticed his hands resting comfortably in his lap. They were wrinkled and worn to the point of having a rough texture. A patchwork of notable scares from a lifetime of living made his hands look used. His hands were a stark contrast to the beauty that was on display all around him. Jack's hands served as a coarse reminder that not all of what he enjoyed about autumn was beautiful or easy. There were plenty of hardships to go around as well. Scratching out a living on a farm is not for the tender hearted.

Jack took notice of the forest below him. Wildlife was buzzing with urgent behavior. Many squirrels were collecting and hiding nuts. Other squirrels were padding their nest with leaves and tree bark. He saw birds nervously flitting from trees and bushes finding seeds and bugs to consume before the coming weeks would soon usher in the cold, baron days of winter.

Jack thought about how there was something very necessary and urgent about the fall season. How it was important to take advantage of autumn's bountiful harvest of fruits, seeds and nuts to prepare for the instinctive harsh environment that would soon arrive. Ducks, geese and other birds were migrating south. Some animals like deer were frantically rutting as if it were important to hurry and get the activity out of their system. Many animals were constructing dens and nest. Meanwhile all of nature was urgently filling food and fat reserves to survive the harsh season to come. It occurred to Jack that maybe God made autumn beautify to camouflage the hardships that were necessary for sustaining your existence.

Jack grew up in a time where it did not matter if you were a creature of the forest or a human, survival and the preparation for continued existence was part of everyday life. And while life may have been simple, it was never easy. Fields had to be cleared, planted and harvested. Livestock were constantly tended and managed. There was always something to shuck, shell, peel, snap, cut, can, nail and tie with a hay string when all else failed. Jack's life was about understanding Mother Nature, reading her signs, surviving by his wit and whatever backbone he could extort out of his body every day without total collapse. While times were not quite so hard anymore, he still believed it was a person's duty to understand the circle of life and your place in it.

Sitting quietly looking out across the horizon, Jack soon started to experience a feeling of discontent. Jack started to dwell on the realization of how much things have changed. People have changed. Technology had changed. Times in general have changed. More importantly, Jack had not changed enough.

He thought about how basic and simple life used to be. Feeling somber, almost apologetic for having lived too long, Jack was thinking how the world, as he knew it, no longer existed. How life, living, surviving always made perfect sense and fit together like a jigsaw puzzle. Man, animals, and the natural environment used to coexist in harmony. The way people went about living their lives now made no sense to him.

He thought about how in today's modern world, harvest means shopping. Food and clothes are but a short drive to the nearest mall or was a computer keyboard stroke away. Experiencing a hardship now-a-days means your cell phone battery has died.

Seed and fertilizer are diligently applied to your lawn instead of your garden of fruits and vegetables. Hunting used to be considered a respectable skill accepted and valued by society as a way to provide for your family. But it wasn't those things that Jack found tragic. It was the ultimate breakdown of husband and wife, child and adult, God and community, right and wrong, and the moral fiber that used to hold it all together that concerned Jack the most.

To Jack, modern society was in trouble. He saw how people worked hard to have material things that did not make them happy. Children were bored and labeled as having attention deficit disorder. The name itself, "attention deficit" suggest to Jack that young people did not have enough work and responsibility to occupy their time. More and more teenagers needed sex and drugs to "find themselves" and to be "accepted" among their peers. Every new generation finds a way to show more skin and talk with a language more rebellious than the last. Society in general was a breeding ground for disrespect disguised as individual rights hidden behind the cloak of social conformity.

None of this modern world stuff mad sense to Jack anymore. His own children have been lured away from living a wholesome, basic lifestyle by modern conveniences and fancy technical innovations. Society seemed to go out of its way to tell Jack that his world did not exist anymore. City folks were buying up all the country land to build neighborhoods and strip malls. It was now more politically correct to fight for animal rights instead of human rights. Somewhere, someone Jack has never met before was trying to take his guns away in the name of being civilized.

Jack's despair was compounded by the fact that he could not fight back. Change, for better or worse, rolled over the landscape like a wildfire. There was nothing anyone could do to stop it. The more he spoke out against change the more he was labeled as an extremist. Jack worried about what kind of world was being handed down to his grandchildren. Would they be able to understand the new social construct any better than he?

What astounded Jack was how many people had no idea where milk and eggs actually came from anymore. Seemed like the more and more people drifted away from toiling the earth with their own hands the more they were removed from the wholesome, basic way of life Jack considered essential for independent survival. Jack once heard it said that ignorance is bliss. He thought if that were true, there must be a lot of very happy people running around in shopping malls using their smart phones with shopping bags stuffed under each arm.

Jack noticed how the afternoon shadows had become long and dim. Direct light rays had been extinguished and now only the bright colors of orange and yellow illuminated the outer most portion of the western sky. With the fading light came the night sounds. Jack remembered how these mysterious night sounds used to frighten him as a young boy. Without conscientious effort, Jack pulled his jacket together at the collar clutching it with one hand as he embraced the breeze with his cheek. Closing his eyes he reveled in the memories of his past. Long ago years that only existed now deep within his soul. He took a deep breath and allowed the cool air to fill his lungs completely before slowly exhaling. Jack realized that his simple way of life was never coming back. Jack felt small and insignificant. He felt that he too would soon be forgotten like the falling leaves blowing in the wind.

The smell of smoke wafting on the breeze from a distant fireplace reminded Jack of warmth and comfort. He eased back and watched as the beautiful colors of the leaves slowly turned a faded gray in the dimming light of the setting sun. Jack could not change the world, but he thought it would be enough if he could impact the people around him. Jack felt privileged to be a living example of everything that was good, wholesome and decent from a time that would soon be a historical bookmark.

If living life the best way he knew how meant being labeled as different, then it was a distinction he was proud to own. Jack felt energized and beamed with renewed purpose. He had lived his whole life never having been a quitter and his stubborn pride was not about to let him go away insignificant. It was important to Jack that his life not be lived for nothing. He wanted to pass along and share with others his unique knowledge and wisdom that had been forged from a lifetime of experiences walking in shoes only his feet had worn.

Jack raised his stiff chin to the wind proclaiming victory over the strife that had been building inside him. Tomorrow was Thanksgiving and he would soon be in the company of his two daughters and three grandchildren. All of them will take turns sitting in his lap fighting for his attention. He will tell them stories about the "old times" and talk about the adventures of his past with excitement and enthusiasm.

While Jack will never really know if he was able to touch their young lives, his simple, modest, and hardworking heritage would indeed greatly impact everyone who was privileged to know him; and someday his life would be celebrated and raised in honorable memory forever known as a great man who lived life the way it used to be.

Meet the Author

Jim's active imagination likely took root in a place called Hell Hole Swamp. (Look it up, it's a real place.) The rural countryside and the unique cultural experiences of his youth were just as colorful as the name of the swamp where he grew up. His love for being outdoors and communing with nature no doubt stem from his persistent forays into the ancient wilderness he called home. Time has a way of disappearing and memories fade. But there are some things in a person's life that are ingrained into their soul and can never be forgotten. Jim's unique foundation was naturally shaped by the good people and clannish social construct found in that swamp. It is this simple country perspective and colorful legacy that comes through in the stories of this book. A legacy he is proud to own and share with you.

Printed in the USA
CPSIA information can be obtained
at www.ICGtesting.com
JSHW051716140124
55292JS00006BA/19